Mystery J

Jeffries

An artistic way to go

3205000235020202

AN ARTISTIC WAY TO GO

AN ARTISTIC WAY TO GO

AN INSPECTOR ALVAREZ NOVEL

Roderic Jeffries

St. Martin's Press
New York

Library of Congress Cataloging-in-Publication Data

Jeffries, Roderic.
    An artistic way to go : an Inspector Alvarez novel /
Roderic Jeffries.
        p.   cm.
    ISBN 0-312-15472-0
    1. Alvarez, Enrique (Fictitious character)—Fiction.
2. Police—Spain—Majorca—Fiction.   I. Title.
PR6060.E43A9   1997
823'.914—dc21   97-7193
                                                              CIP

First published in Great Britain by Collins Crime,
an imprint of HarperCollins*Publishers*

First U.S. Edition: June 1997

10   9   8   7   6   5   4   3   2   1

To Ursula Graham

AN ARTISTIC WAY TO GO

CHAPTER 1

Cooper dropped the copy of *The Times* on to his lap and stared into unfocused distance. Until seeing the date on the paper – which was yesterday's – he had forgotten that this was the second anniversary of Davina's death. If there were an afterlife which provided a window on to earth, she must be in danger of drowning in her own bile; not only on account of Rachael, but because she had been naive enough to believe that good was always rewarded, evil, punished.

He heard the sitting-room French windows click and turned to see Rachael. She was wearing a dress full of chic which underlined without overstating. Even a eunuch would be attracted to her, he thought with possessive satisfaction.

She came up to where he sat, only partially in the shade of the sun umbrella. 'You're going to get burned, Bunnikins.'

'I'm fine.'

'But the sun's a furnace today. And only yesterday there was that programme warning about the harm of too much sun. It would be so terrible if . . .'

He normally argued as a means of self-assertion, but now he stood, moved the chair fully under the shade.

'I know I worry too much about you, but . . .' Leave a man to fill in the missing words and he would always choose those that most flattered him. 'Muriel's just been on the phone. She's asked me to go and have tea with her.'

'More like a double brandy. Why's she always wanting you to go round to her place?'

'I suppose it's because I seem to be able to cheer her up.'

'What's she miserable about this time?'

'She's run up an overdraft and the bank's pressing for immediate repayment as they're not supposed to let her overdraw. She's phoned her husband and asked for a little extra this month, but he won't play. Can you imagine a man in his position refusing to let her have just a couple of hundred pounds?'

'What can she expect when she left him and a couple of kids to go off with an Italian gigolo?'

'I thought he was a count?'

'Same thing.'

'Why don't you like Italians?'

'They're the most crooked art dealers in the world.'

'But I'll bet they never managed to take *you* for a ride?'

'I wasn't born yesterday,' he said complacently.

She rested a hand on his shoulder, stroked the side of his neck with her thumb. 'You're so smart that someone would have to be a genius to put anything over you.'

He agreed.

She removed her hand. 'You don't really mind if I go along and see Muriel, do you?'

'Are you forgetting we're having dinner with the Passmores?'

'I'll be back in plenty of time; promise.'

'You can wear that dress I bought you.'

She giggled. 'That'll upset Edith! The last time we saw her, she moaned that I was always wearing something new.'

'She's bitching because they've lost a packet on Lloyd's and can't get used to having to watch the pennies.'

'Poor dears.'

'Fools not to have foreseen the danger.'

She bent down and kissed him lightly on the cheek. 'Thank goodness you could never do anything so silly, Bunnikins.'

He watched her return into the house. Memory took him back to their first meeting. The day had started with Davina even more morose and argumentative than usual.

The traffic had been so bad that a fifteen-minute drive had taken twenty-five; a fax had arrived during the night to announce that an American sale was off despite its having looked so certain; Mrs Something-or-other had phoned to say that he'd be very sorry to hear her daughter, due to start work with him that morning, had suffered a road accident and the extent of her injuries was not yet known and so she could not be certain when . . . At which point the woman had started snivelling. He'd phoned an agency and asked for a temporary personal assistant/secretary. Rachael had arrived at the gallery that afternoon . . .

His championing of Poperen had proved he was a man who could discern value where others failed to see it. She had been dressed and made up like a tart; had spoken with a Mancunian accent; her manners had betrayed her back-street origins, being in turn gauche, ingratiating, and antagonistic . . . Yet he had identified the gold beneath the dross. One week later, he'd offered her a permanent job.

Maturity offered one big advantage over youth, it enabled a man to move carefully. The selling of art had taught him the truth in the old saying, softlee, softlee, catchee monkee, so for a while he had behaved with complete decorum. Then, knowing from the subtle signs which a man of experience learned to identify that she was attracted to him, he had begun to move. His initial love-making was gentle, but it still left her perturbed by the rush of emotion it aroused in her breast . . . Irritatingly, though, not sufficiently aroused. Despite the gifts, the expensive restaurants, and a technique that was second to none, she'd denied him the final prize. One night, when frustration had overwhelmed him, he'd lost his temper. Tearfully, she'd tried to explain. Because she'd been brought up by very old-fashioned parents, she had ingested very old-fashioned principles. When he touched her breasts (she confessed he was the first man ever to caress her bare breasts) he set fire to her body and she yearned to discover the pleasures in full, but her parents had taught her that adultery was a sin even greater than fornication and so her mind forbade what her body hungered for.

The knowledge that the prize had never been won by anyone else sharpened his already sharp desire, but she had met even his most determined assaults with the same tearful yet steely resolve. Until she was married, she could not allow herself to be taken . . .

Davina had fallen downstairs and died four days later in hospital. The police had been aggressively suspicious, especially when they'd uncovered his friendship with Rachael, but lacking any proof that he'd been near the house at the time, they'd had to accept his innocence.

He'd married Rachael as soon as decency permitted. He'd undertaken her education, teaching her how to behave. His own Eliza. She'd proved to be an adept pupil. By the time he'd sold the gallery and they'd moved to the island, no one, with the possible exception of Muriel, had the slightest suspicion that Rachael's background was even more humble than his had been. And the only reason he thought Muriel might have guessed was that one evening, when she'd drunk even more than usual and had become exceptionally obnoxious, she'd said something that had made him wonder if she were laughing at him . . .

He heard the French windows open a second time and turned to see Rosa step out on to the patio. A fortnight ago, slightly drunk, Bill had confided that if he were Pooh, she was one honey pot he'd be after exploring. It was not the crudeness which had offended, but the thought of lowering oneself to pursue a servant.

She came to a stop a metre from his chair, the harsh sunshine adding to her ripe, earthy attraction, rather than subtracting from it. 'Coffee, señor?' She spoke English with difficulty and much eccentricity. 'And sponge strawberry?'

'Yes, please.' He had not tried to learn Castilian, let alone Mallorquin. The natives spoke English readily enough when they wanted his money.

'Grand. Small?' She moved her hands to illustrate different sizes.

Clara, who did the cooking, made a sponge cake so light it almost had to be tethered. 'A big slice.'

She nodded, returned into the house.

Her novio was slim and raffish and rode a large Yamaha at ferocious speeds. Rosa said his father owned a couple of hotels in Playa Neuva and possessed many, many pesetas. To learn how rich some of the locals were was to understand that the world had become turned upside down.

The cordless phone, lying on the undershelf of the table, rang. He reached down and picked it up, raised the short aerial. 'Yes?'

'It's Charles. I do hope I'm not interrupting anything?'

'You're bound to be interrupting something, aren't you?' he said with heavy humour.

'I'm sorry.'

He had only contempt for people who were forever apologizing.

'I've been wondering if you've heard any more?'

'About what?'

'The latest painting.'

'Not a word. I told you, I'll be in touch if there's anything to be in touch about.'

'Yes, I know, but . . . Well, it is rather a long time now.'

'Surely you learned long ago that in the art world, money is time? My contact is one of the best in the business and he does have a potential buyer in his sights, but the man never makes up his mind in a hurry and it can prove fatal to try to rush him. However, if you want, I'll tell my contact to try to put on a touch of pressure; but then be prepared for the buyer to fade.'

'Obviously, it's best not to take the risk.'

'Quite.'

'I'll just keep my fingers crossed.'

'And your legs, if that doesn't get too painful. Now you're on the phone, you do remember we're leaving a week today, don't you? You'll keep an eye on things as usual?'

'Yes, of course.'

11

'The gardener's growing even lazier than usual and will probably try not to hoover the pool every other day, so be prepared to kick him hard. And if the MacMillans say they're sure we wouldn't mind them using the pool whilst we're away, you can tell them I've said we'd mind very much. If they want to swim in a pool, they can build their own.'

'I'll remember . . . There is one more thing.'

'What?'

'I'm well into my latest painting and I'm sure I've managed to put an extra something into it. One can see the pain as well as the pleasure.'

'Stick to pleasure. People only buy pain when the painter's history.'

'Still, I would be very grateful if you'd have a look at it and give me your opinion.'

'I've much too much on my plate at the moment. I'll let you know when to bring it along.'

'That's very kind.'

'My middle name's Santa.' Cooper cut the call, replaced the phone on the shelf under the table. Despite a working life in art, he was still surprised that a man could be so devoid of artistic judgement as Field was where his own work was concerned.

CHAPTER 2

As Field replaced the receiver, he thought how ironic it was that he should be optimistic when pessimism was warranted. He knew how slowly and tortuously the art world moved, yet before the call he'd inexplicably convinced himself that he was going to hear good news. Still, he hadn't received actual bad news. The potential buyer was still there. It wasn't the financial success he longed for, it was the artistic success that would prove Mary's faith in his work had been justified.

He turned and as he did so his gaze was caught by the photograph of Mary in the elaborate silver frame that had been a wedding present. It had been taken some ten years after their marriage and she was smiling, apparently happy and contented. Impossible to guess that a month before she had been told by the specialist that there was no point in continuing with the fertility treatment. She had longed for children, yet learned she could not have any with quiet acceptance, determined to get the best out of life.

He'd once read that there was a limit to pleasure, but not to pain. That was true. No pleasure could ever be as intense as the degree of mental agony he had suffered when he'd stared down at her in the hospital bed, unable to ease her suffering, willing her death so that she could find peace, dreading her death because that would be the final parting . . .

He crossed the small room of the caseta and stepped through the open doorway. He stared at the fig trees, the stone wall which bounded the field, the small orange grove, and the mountains. He heard sheep bells clanging, dogs barking, and a man singing, his voice carrying a

Moorish intonation. After Mary's death, Cooper had persuaded him that he needed to make a clean break in life and should move out to the island. To his surprise, it had proved to be good advice. Away from the tourist beaches and concrete jungles, the island offered a sense of peace and a link between past, present and future, that allowed a man to regain a reason for living.

He checked the time, turned, shut and locked the front door. Some things had changed even when one was away from the coast. Calvo had told him many times that fifty years before no one had ever bothered to lock up – indeed, the key had been left in view so that others should know one was not at home; now, to leave a door unlocked was to invite theft. Calvo blamed the foreigners for the change, refusing to admit, as was the case, that some of the thieves were Mallorquins, looking for the money to buy drugs. But then, but for the influence of the foreigners perhaps young Mallorquins would have grown up with the same strict standards as their parents had honoured.

He had been no gardener in England – Mary had been the enthusiast – but here he had created a small garden that was colourful throughout the year, helped by advice from Calvo, despite the other's declared belief that the growing of flowers rather than vegetables was a stupid waste of time, effort, and water. He passed several rose bushes, with very few blooms because this was the time of the greatest heat, petunias, hibiscus and plumbago bushes, and stopped briefly in front of a couple of lantanas to watch several hummingbird hawk moths working the flower clusters, their wings a blur of motion and creating a low humming.

The dirt track met a road and he turned on to this and continued along it for a quarter of a kilometre to a narrow lane that had been needlessly tarmacked in the last few weeks, thanks to the grateful, wasteful generosity of the EU.

In the first of Calvo's fields, Marta, dressed in shapeless, faded clothes and wearing a very wide-brimmed straw hat,

14

looked up and shouted a greeting, then continued to irrigate the lines of sweet peppers. He wound his way between tomatoes and aubergines to reach her.

'It's hot enough to make the devil sweat,' she complained.

He still understood far more Mallorquin than he spoke, but the fact that he spoke any was unusual. Most English residents thought it unnecessary, perhaps even demeaning, to learn any more Castilian than was necessary to order red or white wine and they consigned Mallorquin to the natives. But arriving on the island with no inbuilt assumption of superiority and possessed of the unusual belief that a man whose way of life was simple compared to his own was not necessarily stupid, he had decided that having come to live in someone else's country, he should try to master the language. It had proved to be a hard task. Age might enlarge one's wisdom, but it diminished one's ability to learn. But he had persevered, his determination strengthened by the obvious gratification his efforts gave the Mallorquins.

She used the mattock to lift out a sod of earth and allow water to flow from the main irrigation channel into a dry side channel, dropped the earth to plug the filled one. 'He's with the sheep in the olive field.'

'I'll go up there.'

'And when you return, you'll have a drink.'

'Please don't bother . . .'

'You visit without having a drink? You think we are Galicians?' She straightened up and stared at him, then had hurriedly to return to her work as the water overflowed the side channel.

He left her and walked towards the house. Time and again, he'd heard the foreigners, and particularly the English, refer to the Mallorquins as crude, money-grubbing liars. Not one of those critics had ever realized how ignorant of the local life this criticism showed him to be. The Mallorquin manners suited their simplified style of life and were not intended for drawing-rooms with Sheraton chairs and Baluchi rugs; their undoubted love of money arose from the fact that it was not so very long since they had had none; they did not lie, unless they were lawyers, they merely told their listeners what those listeners obviously wished to hear because there was no greater kindness one could offer a man than to make him happy. Great would be the surprise of the critics to learn that Mallorquins considered some of their habits extremely bad mannered . . .

Built out of rock, Mallorquin cement, and Roman roof tiles, the oblong house could not have been of simpler construction yet more adapted to its task, which was no more than to house both humans and animals. Foreigners who bought old farmhouses and reformed them so often destroyed their character by failing to see any merit or beauty in simplicity.

He followed the path round the west side of the house and through a field that had been stubble for weeks and would grow nothing until the winter because it could not be irrigated. Beyond the wide gateway in the stone wall was rising, rough land that became increasingly strewn with boulders, between which grew only weed grasses, brambles, and wild cistus.

At the end of the path was an almost flat area of two hectares on which grew rows of olive trees, the trunks of many so twisted that a fanciful mind could believe they had been frozen in a moment of torment. Beneath the trees, Mallorquin sheep – the lambs were coloured chestnut-brown – grazed the grass which grew thanks to a spring which defied all logic and flowed in the summer to disappear in the winter.

A black and white sheepdog came racing across to greet him, putting its paws up on his chest and ignoring the shouts to get down. As he crossed the field to where Calvo stood under the shade of a tree, it kept nudging his leg, asking for its ears to be fondled. Working dogs were awarded little overt affection.

Calvo studied him. 'You look rough,' he said, with typical directness and disregard for finer feelings.

16

'It's very hot.'

'What d'you expect in July?'

'Also, I am very old.'

'You don't top me by more'n a couple of years and I climb up here without collapsing.'

Calvo was fit enough to climb up Puig Major and not be out of breath, Field thought. Sun and wind had sculpted a face with deep lines of stubborn strength, a life of physical toil had kept his body hard.

Calvo squinted as he looked up at the sun to judge the time. 'They've had long enough. We'll take 'em down.' He whistled, jerked his thin olive staff to the right. The dog went off to the left. He shouted a string of obscenities, cursing the dog and its ancestors. It turned and looked at him, tongue hanging over the side of its mouth as it panted, and Field could believe it was laughing. More shouting and a raised staff persuaded it to do as originally ordered and it worked with skill. The sheep and lambs were collected and herded through the gateway and down the slope to the first field, where they spread out, optimistically searching the stubble for something more to eat.

The two continued on to the house and the patio on the south side, which was protected from the sun by an old vine that grew over a framework of rusty wire stretched between concrete pillars. Three wooden chairs were set around a table that had been made from nailing the side of a packing case to a three-foot length of trunk from an evergreen oak. A casual observer would probably have looked at the table and chairs, at the gaps between the rocks in the wall of the house where the cement had crumbled away, at the shutters with broken or missing slats, and have concluded that the occupants lived at, or even below, the poverty line. It would have been a very wrong conclusion. As did farmers in other countries, the Calvos lived well but would always deny this because in their youth they had experienced poverty, and they would never spend money unless and until it was absolutely necessary to do so.

They sat. The dog settled at Field's side and nudged his legs.

'Carolina will be with us tomorrow because her mother goes to Palma for the day,' Calvo said.

'I'd like to see her. May I?'

At that moment, Marta came into sight around the corner of the house, trailing the mattock as if she were drained of every ounce of energy. 'Hey, old woman, listen to this!' Calvo shouted. 'He asks if he can come and see Carolina tomorrow. He *asks!*'

She looked at Field, her brown eyes expressing puzzlement.

'I was . . .' He wanted to say, 'being polite', but the concept was not one he was able to put directly into Mallorquin. 'It is customary for us to ask. That is polite.'

Calvo's annoyance was not appeased. 'You think you have to be polite? Do you know what Elena will say when I tell her that you ask permission to come and see Carolina? She will say that your head contains more feathers than a chicken's.' He swung round to face Marta. 'Where's the wine?'

'In the usual place.'

'Fetch it.'

She propped the mattock by its handle against one of the concrete pillars, and went into the house.

Calvo reached into his mop of wiry, curly grey hair and scratched the top of his head. 'Does Elena ask if she can come here? Does Carolina? . . . Of course they bloody well don't because they are family.' He slammed his hand down on the table. 'Have I not told you that you are family?'

'You have.'

Marta came out of the house, carrying an earthenware jug in one hand and two glasses in another. She put the glasses down on the table, filled them. Then she faced Field. 'You will eat with us.'

Calvo drank deeply, wiped his mouth with the back of his hand. 'He is family, yet he asks! Truly, only a fool can be stupider than a lost sheep.'

18

As Field sipped the rough wine that would have had any connoisseur searching for a spittoon, he experienced a rush of emotion towards the two that was a form of love. They had lived through hard, occasionally terrible, times and this had taught them that the only certainty, and therefore the most precious thing in the world, was family. So when they said he was family, they were offering him the greatest gift that was theirs to give. How many people were ever prepared to do that?

CHAPTER 3

Rachael looked at her watch. 'I must leave in quarter of an hour. We've just time.'

'For what?' Burns asked.

'You need two guesses? What's the trouble – no imagination or no stamina?'

'Imagination to spare and stamina for six.'

'So prove you're something more than a big mouth.'

He did.

Afterwards, he lay on the bed as he watched her dress. 'When are you off on this bloody cruise?'

'On the nineteenth.' About to step into a pair of lace-edged pants, she paused, turned. 'And make a good note of this. You start entertaining the tourists whilst I'm away and I'll castrate you.'

'One law for the rich, another for the poor. I have to lead a life of celibacy, while you're wearing yourself out.'

'With Oliver? Doing my duty when I have to, which, thank God, isn't very often these days.'

'Not as athletic as he was?'

'The track's become too soft for records.' She pulled up her pants, looked at her watch. 'Dammit, I'll be late.'

'You said I was to use my imagination . . . Anyway, what's the panic?'

'We're going out to dinner and he wants to leave sharp at a quarter to eight.'

'He must be the only person on the island who worries about arriving on time.'

'He was born pedantically.'

'Who are you noshing with?'

'The Passmores.'

'The couple with a yacht almost the size of the *QE2*?'

'He wouldn't like to hear the "almost".'

'Why waste your time with the likes of them? She's a bitch.'

'In my vocabulary, the biggest bitch on the island.' She picked up her dress from the back of a chair. 'And is that saying something!'

'It sounds as if she's been looking at you through her lorgnette.'

'Very droll.'

'Why don't you stick two fingers up at her?'

'And give Oliver another ulcer? They're so rich that if they told him Monet was a lousy artist, he'd rush to agree.'

'Your husband's a creep.'

'Who's arguing?'

'Divorce him and marry me and learn what life can be like.'

'I learned that before I married him and didn't know how to pay the electricity bill.'

'Money's all-important?'

'Lack of it is.'

'I've told you, I'll make the grade.'

'Call again when you do.'

'You're not so backward at being a bitch!'

'Look, love, get down off your high horse and be practical. If I divorced Oliver, he'd do everything in his power to make me suffer and leaving me penniless would be for starters. As much as you and me see life the same way, we'd start rowing if the money dried up. Two people never did live as cheaply as one.'

'Then we just go on like now, seeing each other when you can snatch a couple of hours away from his pot belly?'

'That's right.'

'Exciting!'

'Why get so steamed up? Start remembering that Oliver's not as young as he used to be and that he eats too much, drinks too much, and smokes like a chimney.'

'What if he does?'

21

'Men like him have heart attacks by the score. Especially if they're not normally all that active, but are encouraged to become frantic and frenetic.'

'You mean . . . You're beginning to add a whole new dimension to screwing.'

'Think of me as enthusiastic.'

He climbed off the bed, kissed her. 'Think of you as Spanish fly in the night.' He walked over to the chest of drawers on which were several bottles. 'What'll you drink?'

'I told you, I've got to rush.'

He poured himself a gin and tonic. 'If he does die happy, how can you be certain you'll end up all right?'

'I'm the sole beneficiary.'

'He may have told you that, but it could be all balls.'

'I've seen his will.'

'Seeing the kind of man he is, I'm surprised he showed it to you.'

'He didn't. I learned the combination of the wall safe a long time ago.'

He drank. 'I'm learning more about you every day.'

'That'll keep you interested.'

'I don't need artificial aids.'

She went through to the tiny bathroom, checked her image in the mirror, lightly powdered her cheeks, patted an errant hair into place, returned to the main room. 'How do I look?'

'I'd never guess that only a short time ago the earth moved so fiercely for you, you thought there'd been an earthquake.'

'Self-flattery is a sign of insecurity.' She moved forward, ran her hand down his flat, muscled stomach, pinched.

'Why the hell d'you do that?' he shouted, as he jerked back.

'To give you a taste of what will happen if you ever think of straying.' She put on a large pair of dark glasses and left.

*   *   *

22

Had she not been the Right Honourable the Countess Janlin, estranged wife of the seventh earl, a man of vast estate, she would have been cold-shouldered by those expatriates who were alarmed by the unconventional or who believed that a gold or platinum card was the prerequisite to friendship. She lived in a poky, unreformed, Mallorquin house, dressed in what might well have been Oxfam rejects, drove a clapped-out Seat 127, and occasionally had a man to live with her who, on at least one occasion, had been a Mallorquin. But possessed of so exalted a pedigree, the conformists spoke of aristocratic eccentricity and even the richest of the parvenus were quick to declare their liking for her.

When young and often in the news, she had usually been described as possessing the traditional English peaches-and-cream complexion; years of hot sun, brandy, and a wilful refusal to use any skin cream, meant that prune-like was a more apposite description. Her body, once slender and shapely, had thickened and sagged.

She sat in the small garden, listening to a tape recorder that was playing Strauss's 'Don Quixote'. As Rachael opened the gate, she stopped the music. 'The booze is in the usual place.'

Rachael walked caterwise across the patio and on to the lawn of gama grass. 'I don't think I'll have anything.'

'Why not?'

'We're having dinner with the Passmores . . .'

'More fool you.'

Muriel had obviously reached the belligerent stage so it would be stupid to provoke her. 'Maybe just a small one, then.'

'That's not what you'll have been wanting for the past couple of hours. Good, was it?'

'I've no complaints.'

'Then you're bloody lucky! By the time George had finished imitating a rig with a double rupture, I'd nothing but complaints.'

Rachael crossed to the trolley on the patio and poured

herself a weak gin and tonic, added ice, picked up a saucer of baked almonds in their skins. She returned, settled on the second uncomfortable, rusting wrought-iron chair. She raised her glass. 'Cheers.'

'Good God, how many more times do I have to tell you that it's only little people from Bagshot who say "Cheers"?'

She drank. 'Has Oliver rung?'

'No.'

'I told him you were feeling miserable again and needed cheering up.'

'And he swallowed that? There's something to be said for being married to a pompous fool.'

'In some things, you know, he's very far from being a fool.'

'I don't know.'

Rachael looked at her watch. She must leave very soon if she were to arrive home in time to shower and dress and be ready to leave by a quarter to eight.

'Make him wait. Do him good.'

Not for the first time, she wondered why Muriel was so ready to assist in Oliver's cuckolding? Contempt for him? Because he was so much richer than she? Or was it that because her own marriage had turned into farce, she welcomed the chance to assist in wrecking someone else's?

CHAPTER 4

As Serra approached the large cisterna, made from blocks of sandstone, there were no sounds of flowing water. He swore. He continued past two kumquat trees to the north-east corner of the cisterna, climbed up on to the wall, using rocks which had been extended to form rough steps, and stared down at the narrow aqueduct, also fashioned from sandstone, which ran along the top of it. The channel was dry so the water had flowed for only a short time or not at all. He moved carefully along the top of the wall, legs straddling the channel, until he could look down into the cisterna. The level of water was very low.

He studied the sky, beginning to lose its intensity of colour, hoping to see rain clouds, even though there had been no rain for weeks and would be none for at least another month; if he hadn't been an optimistic pessimist, he wouldn't have been a farmer.

How many days' water was left in the cisterna? Not nearly enough. Even though he knew it would infuriate him to do so, he turned and stared into the garden of Ca'n Oliver. The riot of colour should have warmed his heart, but it made him swear afresh. All those flowers, all that lawn, existed only because he was being denied the water he needed to grow his vegetables and fruit.

It was his brother's fault. His brother was a good-for-nothing who'd lost to the roll of three dice his half of the land which had been left by their father; he'd have gambled away his wife if anyone were fool enough to accept so sharp-tongued a bitch as a stake. The land had been bought by a German, immensely rich as were all foreigners, who'd built a large house and swimming pool and ordered the rich land to be turned into a garden which needed the water that God had intended should grow food. But the German had been reasonable – for a foreigner, that was. He'd never complained when the aqueduct had not flowed, had never questioned why he was not receiving the water to which he was entitled, but instead had bought what was needed by the lorryload. So he, Serra, had received all the water instead of just half, enabling him to increase production.

Then the German had died, the property had been sold, and it had been bought by another foreigner (no Spaniard could be so bereft of brains as to pay the kind of money that had been asked; not even a politician). He had naturally imagined Señor Cooper would honour the existing arrangement. If only the señor had proved to be even half the man the German had been! On learning that owner-ship of the land entitled him to sixteen and a half hours' of water a week, he had demanded this. When the aque-duct had remained dry, he'd called in a pompous, self-opinionated abogado – was there any other kind? – who had ordered him to stop diverting to his own use water to which he was not entitled. He ignored the order, of course. So the abogado – no honest Mallorquin but from the Penin-sula – had threatened legal action and had spoken to Fer-nando Gelabert, who lived near the mouth of the valley and was in charge of the system of distribution and had warned that if his client didn't receive his correct allotment, Gelabert would be stripped of his honorary position . . .

Desperate problems demanded desperate remedies. He'd spent a great deal of money on a bottle of the strongest weedkiller which one night he'd poured into the señor's cisterna. Yet no flowers had withered, no tree had shed its leaves, the lawn had not turned brown and, even though they used that water to top up the swimming pool, neither the señor nor the señora had been stricken with the pox. (She was a puta. Jorge had told him many times that she swam in the nude.) He'd melted down a candle and from the soft wax modelled a figure upon which he'd urinated

26

as he christened it Señor Oliver; he'd heated five needles and stuck them into the figure, one in each eye, one in the centre of the stomach, and one in each testicle, yet during the succeeding days the señor had not been blinded, doubled up with his stomach on fire, or walked as if on hot bricks.

In desperation, he'd allowed the water to flow into the señor's cisterna for long enough to make any reasonable man think all was well, then diverted it into his own. Jorge had known what was happening, but he was a friend as well as a Mallorquin. Yet that bastard of a señor had not only checked to make certain the water was running at the beginning of each period, he'd also checked later on. Now Jorge only occasionally dared turn a blind eye other than when the señor was away . . .

He climbed down the wall and followed the path around the cisterna, came to a stop. The land sloped away so that he could look out over his crops. Beans, peas, tomatoes, lettuces, sweet peppers, aubergines, cucumbers, radishes, grapes, oranges, lemons, grapefruit, almonds, figs, persimmons . . . Nowhere on the island grew larger, sweeter, juicier, tastier fruit and vegetables. When his wife set up her stall in the market, the Mallorquins rushed to buy from her before the long-abed foreigners arrived and willingly paid whatever was asked. But if he could not find a way of once more obtaining all the water he needed for such heavy cropping, he would either have to reduce the amount he grew or buy water. The first would make other farmers snigger, the second, laugh.

He lived in the village, not far from the old square, in one of the original, twisting roads that wound its way part way up the conical hill about which Llueso was built. The house had not been reformed beyond the installation of a modern flushing lavatory, as demanded by the ayuntamiento – like all bureaucrats, they spent other people's money with gay abandon.

He looked across the kitchen, which was also their dining- and sitting-room. 'I'm going to see Jorge.'

Ana nodded. Years of working in the fields in sun and wind had left her with a complexion of leather, a thickset, muscular body, and rheumatism and arthritis.

'He'll help.'

'If he can.' She seldom said more than was necessary.

He went through to the front room and out on to the road that was so narrow that however considerately a car parked, it caused problems to moving vehicles. At the bottom, a flight of stone steps led down at the point where the road turned sharp left. The steps ended almost directly opposite a bar that was popular because it had not been modernized, and it retained the air of shabbiness that deterred any but the most determined foreigner in search of local colour. He spoke to the owner behind the bar. 'Has Jorge been in?'

'Not yet.'

'Give me a coñac.'

Some minutes later, Barcelo, considerably younger than he, entered, crossed to where he sat on a stool. 'How are things with you?'

'No worse than usual.'

Barcelo ordered a drink. 'Is it right you're retiring?'

'What bloody fool's saying that?'

'The story's not true?'

'What story?'

'The English señor is so angry over you pinching his share of the water that he's going to court to ask for all the water for the next three years to make up for what he's lost.'

'Where d'you hear that?'

'It's only fair.'

'You call it fair, him using it for his garden and pool?'

'If it's his, he can do what he wants with it.'

'It belongs to the land.'

'It'll belong to him when the court says. Your old woman won't have anything to sell in market 'cept a few almonds

28

and figs.' Barcelo sniggered as he took the glass and bottle of beer he was handed. 'But I'm a generous kind of a bloke. I'll find you a job. Even pay you what you're worth . . . Ten pesetas an hour.'

'Which is ten more than you've ever earned honestly.' Serra stood, crossed to one of the tables, sat. He saw Barcelo talk to the owner, whereupon both men laughed. Rejoicing at his coming misfortunes. The story had to be nonsense, born of bitter jealousy. Yet . . . yet the señor had proved himself time and again to be ignorant of the customs of the countryside and if he were egged on by a lawyer whose ambition was to retire richer than the clients he swindled . . . In his mind, he saw his land deprived of all water; the vegetables withered, the fruit rotting on the ground because the trees could no longer support their crops . . .

Amoros entered and ordered a glass of wine. Short and stocky, his character was as phlegmatic as his heavy, lined face suggested. He crossed and sat opposite Serra.

Serra leaned forward. 'Barcelo says the English señor is going to ask the court to award him all the water for three years to make up for what he thinks I've been having. That can't be right, can it?'

Amoros drank.

'Well, can it?'

'Who's to know what a foreigner's going to do, especially the likes of him.' He brought a battered pack of Ducados out of his pocket, lit a cigarette.

'But you've heard nothing?'

He shook his head.

'You must have done if it was true?'

He shrugged his shoulders.

There was a long silence, broken by Serra. 'You cut off the water earlier.'

'The señor saw it wasn't running and sent Rosa to tell me to alter the flow. Even followed me to make certain I did that. Don't trust no one. 'Cept his wife, which shows how stupid he is. She swims in the nude.'

'So you've said often enough.'

'If I was younger, it'd make me think hard. Last time, she wasn't on her own. The man wasn't in a costume either. Only whilst I was watching, they didn't do anything,' he added regretfully.

'Try again.'

Amoros sniggered. 'Maybe that's what she was saying to him.'

Serra thought for a while, his heavy brow furrowed, his eyes unfocused. 'Suppose I was to go to the señor and tell him. You steal my water and I'll tell you something that'll make you wish you'd never started?'

'He'll laugh in your face.'

'He'll stop laughing when I tell him about the señora.'

'Do that and he'll really like you, won't he? Like as not, ask the court to have your share of the water for six years.'

'I'm not going to let him have what's mine for a single day,' Serra said fiercely.

Barcelo, who'd been about to leave, paused in the doorway. 'Don't forget – ten pesetas.' He laughed as he went out into the street.

'His father was just as much of a bastard,' Serra said, indicating the doorway. 'Fifteen years back I lent him my mule for a morning and he never paid.'

'When he was buried, the undertaker didn't see the colour of his money for months.'

'So maybe he went down instead of up . . . Not even a foreigner would steal all the water.'

'You don't know the señor. The other day he found I was growing some tomatoes behind the bamboos and he shouted as if I'd been screwing his wife. Made me tear out the bushes; wouldn't even let me pick the ripe ones first,' Amoros said bitterly.

'He's bloody mad.'

'Mad or not, it's his land and his water.'

Serra swore.

CHAPTER 5

Cooper, enjoying the cool of the air-conditioned sitting-room, looked puzzled. 'Who rang?'

'Ernest White,' Rachael replied.

'I don't know anyone by that name.'

'From the way he was talking, he knows you. He'll be along at twelve.'

Cooper scratched the crown of his head, then automatically smoothed down his hair that was thinning far more rapidly than he'd admit. 'Why didn't you find out exactly who he is and what he wants? He could be that blasted representative of some financial advisory service who's going around the island, touting for business.'

'He didn't sound like a salesman.'

'That's the art of being a salesman.' He began to tap on the arm of the chair with the fingers of his right hand. 'Educated?'

'I forgot to ask him if he had a degree.'

'There's no need to be facetious,' he said ponderously.

She silently swore at herself. The last thing she wanted right then was for him to become annoyed and resentful.

'Where was he speaking from?'

'He didn't say.'

'And you didn't ask?'

She didn't answer.

'You are certain he didn't give you any indication at all of why he wanted to see me?'

'Positive.'

'You should have told him to phone back later, when I'd returned from the village.'

'Please don't be so angry, Bunnikins. I try so hard to do

the right thing, but I know I don't always succeed. We can't all be like you.'

'I suppose not,' he agreed, his annoyance lessened by the inference that few men were as smart as he.

'Forgive?'

'Try to do better next time.'

She came forward and kissed him, straightened up. 'I'm going to nip into the village.'

'Why?'

'I need to buy some women's things.' The reference embarrassed him, as she'd intended, since this made certain he would not pursue the matter. There were aspects of life he found distasteful, since he was a man of great artistic sensibility, and what he didn't like, he ignored. 'And after shopping, I thought I'd just drop in at Muriel's to say goodbye.'

'But you saw her yesterday.'

'Yes, I know. She was so terribly miserable, though, and I'd like to cheer her up a little if I can. The bank won't cash her cheques now and so she rang her husband again, but the beastly man won't help.'

'As I've said before, why should he?'

'She only went off with the Italian because he spent all his time with his horses and ignored her.'

'It's a wife's duty to honour a husband however he behaves.'

'Isn't that being rather old-fashioned, Bunnikins?'

'When it comes to duty I am proud to say that I am very old-fashioned.'

Troglodytic. 'So it wouldn't matter how you treated me, I'd never be justified in leaving you?'

'Naturally not.'

'And if I did, you'd refuse to give me a penny if I was in financial trouble?'

He looked at her, curious yet not suspicious. 'Have you a particular reason for asking?'

She moved until she could cradle his head against her. 'Of course I haven't. I just like hearing you be so stern and

32

domineering. Didn't you know women love to be dominated?'

He loved dominating. He ran his hand up under her skirt and patted her neat bottom.

She moved away slowly, giving him plenty of time to free his hand. 'I won't stay a moment longer than's necessary. You know that all the time I'm away, I'll be wanting to hurry back to be with you.' There had been moments in the past when she'd suddenly thought she'd gone too far in pandering to his vanity, but recently she'd decided that that was impossible. She ruffled his hair with her hand, left the sitting-room.

He wondered whether to bring an end to her friendship with Muriel by forbidding any further intercourse on her part (an unfortunate choice of words, but that escaped him), but decided not to do so. Whilst it was irritating that she should spend an increasing amount of time in Muriel's company, they had made several contacts as a result of the friendship that were socially of considerable benefit. He nodded. A clever man never reached a decision until he'd assessed all the factors involved and identified where his best interests lay. For the moment, anyway, he'd allow the friendship to continue.

He was watching a satellite television programme about the life and work of Gauguin – full of factual errors and faulty opinions – when Clara stepped into the sitting-room. She spoke in Spanish.

'What is it?' he asked bad-temperedly. Clara annoyed him, first because she was so stupid she spoke no English, secondly because she was so extraordinarily ugly. But she was a very good cook. It was the Higgs – elusive, choosy about their friends, so rich they paid no tax in any country – who had complimented Rachael on serving the best meal they'd had since they'd dined at the Tour d'Argent. One did not lightly sack a cook capable of pleasing uncrowned royalty.

She said the same thing over and over again and

33

eventually he interpreted her babble sufficiently to understand that a Señor White had arrived. 'Show him in.'

As she left, he rose from the chair and went over to the fireplace, to stand in front of it with hands clasped behind his back. A man in command.

White entered. ''Morning, Oliver.' His voice was quiet and smooth, his accent light American.

There was little that riled Cooper more than the modern custom of using Christian names on first acquaintance. Christian names denoted a degree of equality. 'I understand that you are Mr White?'

He smiled, showing even white teeth. 'That's what my parents told me.'

'We've not met before.'

'Correct one hundred per cent.'

White was well dressed – it was uncommon in the middle of the summer for a man to wear a tie and neatly pressed linen suit – and his manner was pleasant, but there was something about him that Cooper found disturbing. His size? He stood six feet three or four inches tall and his build was in proportion. No, it was something more than mere size. Despite himself, Cooper felt the need to tread softly. 'Would you like a drink?'

'A gin and tonic, thanks. Mind if I sit?' He sat. 'You've sure got a nice piece of real estate here.'

'We like it.' Cooper spoke in tones which, hopefully, would damp any enthusiasm if this man turned out to be some kind of estate agent. There were any number of foreigners on the island who tried to make a living by hook or, far more frequently, by crook. He crossed to the cocktail cabinet and opened the doors, which automatically switched on the interior strip lights. He upended two crystal goblets, poured out the drinks.

'Beautiful island. Kind of place a man dreams of retiring to. I guess you're retired?'

The ice bucket was empty. He crossed to the bell push, depressed it.

Clara entered.

'You've forgotten to put out any ice. I've told you again and again, I want ice in the bucket all the time. Are you incapable of carrying out the simplest order?'

She stared at him. 'Señor?'

White spoke rapidly in Spanish. She shrugged her shoulders, left.

'Hope you don't mind?' White said.

'Of course not,' Cooper replied stiffly, knowing he had been made to look foolish.

'Learned Spanish when I was at high school. Probably sounds like Portuguese, but it gets me around.'

'Very useful,' was all Cooper could find to say. 'You haven't explained why you're here.'

'That's right, I haven't. Kind of been too busy envying you. I guess you've turned life just right. A beautiful wife, a lovely house, someone to do all the work – what more can a man want?'

Further annoyed by the impudence of the observation, Cooper was about to comment angrily when Clara returned with a silver ice bucket which she handed to him.

White said something to her and she smiled. Normally, she never smiled. Cooper would have given much to know what White had said, but was damned if he was going to ask. He carried the ice bucket over to the cocktail cabinet, dropped two cubes into each goblet, handed White one goblet, resumed his position in front of the fireplace, even though he had the uneasy impression that he was not cutting the figure he had intended.

White raised his glass. 'The best way to get to know a guy is to have a drink with him. Wouldn't you agree?'

'I can't say I've ever considered the proposition.'

'That's what I like about you Brits. The dignified way you do everything, most of all, speak . . . Now, what do we drink to? A long life if it's a happy one, a short one if it isn't?'

The words were inane, but they seemed to Cooper somehow to carry a threat. He struggled to break free from the growing feeling of disquiet. 'Have you met my wife?'

'I've not had the pleasure.'

'From the way you spoke earlier, I assumed you must have done.'

'It's just that when I've seen her around, I've said to myself, now there's the genuine English rose.'

'But if you've never met her, how could you know what she looks like?'

'I've been watching how things go around here.'

'You've . . . you've been doing what?'

'I always like to learn a little about the life of someone I'm asking to repay a debt.'

'I don't know what the devil you mean by that.'

'I mean, a debt of one million two hundred and fifty grand, plus another hundred grand for expenses and loss of interest.'

'Over a million pesetas . . .'

'Dollars. Payable within the next forty-eight hours.'

'You're crazy.'

'Let's try and make it easier for you to understand. Remember Campbell?'

He searched his brain, but found only chaos.

'He visited your shop and told you he was acting for a buyer who wanted a nice picture, or two.'

Even at such a confused moment, the word 'shop' infuriated him. 'I owned a gallery, not a shop.'

'So where's the difference? He was buying, you were selling.'

'Obviously, there's no point in trying to explain.'

'Then leave me to do the talking. Campbell told you that he wanted quality. You suggested something by a Frenchman because in twenty years' time his work would be worth a whole lot more than was paid. Later on, you sold two paintings for one million two hundred and fifty grand. Now, my principal is asking for his money back. With that extra.'

Memory finally returned. Some time before he'd sold the gallery, Campbell – an American, which had explained his choice in clothes and his brash manner – had appeared

36

and said he represented a client who looked to art as a means of investment. The artistic side of Cooper's character had urged him to point out that a painting should be appreciated for its quality, not its financial potential, but his business instincts had been too strong for him to act on so high-minded an urge. He had taken Campbell to lunch at one of his favourite restaurants. Incredibly, the other had chosen to drink Coca-Cola as an apéritif. The wine waiter had only just managed to conceal his contempt. It would, he had said over the prawn mousse, be necessary first to speak to the actual buyer to ascertain what were his interests, since even if he bought because of investment potential, it was best that he should like the work or works. That, Campbell had said, was unnecessary. Just find something that would make a good investment, up to a million dollars; it was immaterial who the artist, period, and subject were. It sounded doubtful. By the time Cooper was eating the apple and passion fruit flan, liberally coated with whipped cinnamon cream, he had angrily decided that he'd been conned into providing a free and expensive meal.

However, a week later, Campbell had returned. Were the painting or paintings ready? As if art could be bought and sold with the same careless ease as a dozen cases of whisky! But since the other was an American, he had begun to explain that when he received a buying commission he held himself bound in equity as well as contract to conduct the widest possible search in order to identify the best possible buy.

'So get searching,' Campbell had said.

He had coughed a couple of times. Since it would appear that he was not to have direct contact with the principal, he would very much appreciate a guarantee that any expenses properly and necessarily incurred in the search would be reimbursed in the unfortunate event of his not being able to locate what was wanted . . .

Campbell, not possessing a developed sense of decorous business behaviour, had merely produced ten one-hundred-dollar notes and demanded to know if that was good enough? Then he had left, refusing to give any address.

Poperen? His work offered every chance of a very good appreciation in value. Though it would hurt the soul to buy his paintings and know that they were destined to be owned by some Philistine who probably thought Van Dyck was a female new age traveller.

It had begun to seem that, ironically thanks to his own efforts, Poperen's work had become far more appreciated than he had recognized. Because the artist had died young, he had produced a relatively small oeuvre and those who now owned his paintings were seeing the values of these constantly rise and were therefore unwilling to sell until and unless convinced the market had reached a plateau. But finally he had found in Berlin two of the largest works in the hands of a man who had needed money quickly . . .

It was on his return from Berlin, with price and delivery date agreed, that the stewardess, handing out newspapers, had passed him one of the tabloids. He had asked for a broadsheet, preferably *The Times*, but she had said that all copies had already been distributed. With nothing else to read – he'd left a paperback in the hotel by mistake – he had begun to leaf through the paper, the standard of its contents confirming his firm belief that democracy was doomed since even the readers of a paper like this had the vote. Then on one of the pages he'd been surprised and disconcerted to see the photograph of the man whom he'd known as Campbell. The short article accompanying this noted that Ed Murray had been found guilty by a Philadelphia court on three counts of vicious assault, one of which had left a man brain-damaged and blind. According to the prosecution, Murray had been the enforcer for one of the Mafia bosses . . .

He had ordered another gin and tonic. For some years there had been reports of criminals laundering money through art; either buying legitimately or from thieves. Dealers had been asked to inform the authorities should they have any reason to suspect this was happening. So should he now tell the police about Campbell? But had he learned anything of the slightest significance? And therefore it did seem pointless, if one looked at things realistically, to suffer the inevitable hassle . . .

Three weeks later, another American, who gave his name as Sumner, had entered the gallery and asked him if he'd secured the paintings. He'd explained how hard the search had proved, then added that he thought he had found a seller. At the moment, he was trying to persuade the seller to accept a price that was fair to all parties . . .

'Hurry it up,' Sumner had said.

There could no longer be any doubt as to where his duty lay. He'd almost rung the police; almost . . . That night, his thoughts had ranged far and wide. The recession had hit the art world really hard and profits at the gallery had slumped alarmingly. Davina had never been a careful spender, but compared to Rachael, she was a miser. Rachael had taken to the luxury life with an enthusiasm that was breathtaking and pocket-emptying. And when he'd tried to stem the expenses, she had shown, in the subtle way in which a woman did, that his pleasures depended on her pleasures . . .

Paintings bought with black money were not immediately going to be put on display, they were going to be kept under wraps; they would only appear years later when without risk to the owner they could be shown in public as an ego boost or sold to legitimize both capital and profit. So a forgery could be sold to such a buyer in the certain knowledge that it would not be examined by an expert until long after any doubts about authenticity could affect the seller; indeed, even that might not matter since really good fakes were time and again declared to be genuine by experts who were too self-opinionated ever to accept that doubt could be cast on their judgements . . .

Charles Field had been carrying out restoration work all his career and was brilliant at this. Several years back, one of Poperen's paintings had been brought to the gallery by a man who had inherited it from Poperen's niece, because even in France Oliver Cooper was acknowledged to be the expert on the artist's work. The niece had obviously been a very prudish woman because she had banished the painting to an attic and there it had suffered so much from damp and dirt that by the time it reached the gallery, it had been in very poor condition. He'd pointed out all the faults and offered a suitably reduced price and this had been accepted. Then he'd handed the painting to Field and asked for as good a job of restoration as was possible. Field was a slow worker and so it had been months before the painting had been returned, but then it was only with the greatest difficulty that he had been able to make out the restoration work . . . He'd hesitated, then sold it at auction without any caveat and been gratified by the price it fetched . . .

His thoughts were abruptly interrupted.

'I'd say you've finally remembered,' White drawled. 'So now you know why you're being asked to repay the million two hundred and fifty grand, plus, for the fakes.'

'They were nothing of the kind . . .'

'Cut the crap. A couple of months back, my principal had an argument and by the time it was over one of the paintings had been damaged. So he sent it to an expert to be repaired. This expert's a smart guy. Because the tear allowed him to see a cross-section of the paint, something didn't seem quite right; he began to wonder if the painting might just be a fake. So it was X-rayed, microscoped, spectroscoped, put under infrared and ultraviolet, and finally given something called transverse irradiation. The verdict? It was a brilliant fake. So my principal got to thinking and sent the second painting for examination. Same result.

'When a man learns he's spent a million two hundred and fifty thousand for a couple of fakes, he's not smiling. But he's a fair man and understands that maybe you were conned when you bought, just like him. All he's asking is repayment plus that little bit extra.'

'I sold them in good faith.'

'Haven't I just said? So provided the money's ready for

40

electronic transmission this time Tuesday, everything's smooth.'

'But . . . but that's three-quarters of a million pounds.'

'So?'

'I can't find that sort of money.'

'They say that where there's a will, there's a way. Try harder.' White stood. 'Been a pleasure, Oliver. And I'm telling you, if I lived in this lovely house with a beautiful wife, I sure as hell wouldn't want anything to disturb the scene.'

Cooper watched White stride across to the inside door and go out into the hall. After a moment, he heard a car drive off, yet still he seemed to be unable to move. The threat was all the more terrifying because it had never actually been spelled out.

CHAPTER 6

When Dolores stepped through the bead curtain across the doorway from the kitchen, Alvarez and Jaime sat at the dining-room table and Isabel and Juan were lounging in chairs set in front of the television. She was about to speak when Jaime, never one to get his timing right, said: 'Isn't grub ready yet? I'm hungry.'

She put her hands on her hips and held her strongly featured head high, her midnight-black hair providing a handsome corona. 'Should I apologize humbly for the delay?'

'Humbly' was not a word that came readily to her lips. Alvarez tried to express silently that he disassociated himself from Jaime's question.

'It's just . . . Well, I thought . . .' Jaime became silent.

'You have forgotten? I have read many times that alcohol destroys the brain cells.'

'What are you on about?'

'You cannot recall that the gas gave out and I asked you to change the bottle? Or that I had to wait and wait until I could wait no longer or the cooking would be ruined and so I had to struggle to change it myself. Because of that, the meal will not be ready for a little while yet. But perhaps the fault is really mine. No doubt I should have allowed for the fact that when you are drinking, which is for most of the time, you cannot be bothered with anything so unnecessary as helping your wife.' She lowered her hands, turned, swept through the bead curtain and back into the kitchen.

'I'll swear she's getting worse,' Jaime muttered. 'On at me every day. What have I done to deserve that? Nothing.'

42

'That's what she's complaining about,' Alvarez said.

'Bloody funny! . . . I was going to change the gas as soon as I'd finished what I was doing. She expects me to run the moment she speaks. You know why women are like that these days, don't you? It's all that nonsense in the papers and on the telly about them being equal to men. Well, in this house, they aren't. There's only one boss and that's me.' He made certain Dolores wasn't watching through the bead curtains, poured himself a large brandy, added ice. 'She was very different when we were first married. Knew her place. Why do women change so?'

'They can be themselves once they've got all they want.'

'It's bloody unfair.' He drank. 'You're sensible; you've stayed single. You can walk along the beach and stare at all the bare titties and not have to pretend you're looking at something else.'

'That's all right until one gets old.'

'If you've had your fun, it's easier to put up with things. In any case, all you have to do then is look for a widow with property.'

Dolores appeared. 'Is it Adela? Her land was some of the best when Luis, God rest his soul, was alive to farm it. The house in the village needs reformation since he was always so close with the money he'd never have any work done, but being so close there must be very many pesetas under the mattress. She's a good woman. She wore black for a year and now is in grey.' She smiled warmly at Alvarez. 'I have always thought that one day you would mature sufficiently to stop lusting after foreign women who are little more than children.'

Juan looked away from the television, that was showing advertisements. 'What's lusting mean?'

'Behaving like a man,' she answered, her present good humour in sharp contrast to her earlier manner. 'You and Isabel can lay the table.' She returned into the kitchen.

Isabel stood and went round to the sideboard, carved in a traditional pattern, pulled open a drawer and brought out a tablecloth with blue Mallorquin embroidery. 'Clear the table,' she ordered her brother.

'Clear it yourself.'

She turned to Jaime. 'Tell him he's got to do it.'

'It's women's work.' Jaime said to Alvarez: 'She thinks you're after Adela. You aren't, are you?'

'You think I'm that crazy? Luis always said that he'd have been more comfortable living with a porcupine.'

Jaime jerked his thumb in the direction of the kitchen. 'For God's sake don't let on until after the meal.'

For once, Alvarez thought, Jaime had spoken sense. Let her work herself into a full temper and even at this late moment she might deliberately become so careless that the meal was less than perfect. He poured himself another drink.

She carried in plates, returned for an earthenware dish which she set on the earthenware ring in the centre of the table. She lifted the lid and prepared to serve.

Sopa de peix de Sant Telm! Alvarez thought. When made by Dolores, a fish soup to lift up a man to dine with the gods. As he drained his glass and refilled it with wine, he allowed his thoughts to become more charitable. Women had many failings, but there were some whose achievements went a long way towards excusing these.

Members of the Cuerpo General de Policia normally operated from the police stations of the Policia Armada y de Trafico, but some years before and as a temporary measure, Alvarez had been given an office in the Guardia post in Llueso. He had remained in Llueso ever since, an arrangement that suited him since otherwise he'd have been stationed several kilometres away in Playa Nueva and have been unable to return home to lunch.

He settled in the chair behind the desk and pondered the question, What might Dolores have cooked for lunch? It was quite some time since they'd had Greixnera de xot, and if anyone could turn lamb stew into a dish fit to be served in a five-crossed-forks restaurant, she could . . . The

44

telephone rang. Grunting from the effort, he wriggled himself into an upright position and lifted the receiver.

'There's a call for you,' said the duty cabo. 'Some foreign woman can't find her husband.'

'Why not?'

'He's missing.'

'Since when?'

'How should I know?'

'By asking her.'

'That's your job, not mine.' There was a change of tone. 'You're through, señora.'

She said, in Spanish: 'My husband has gone . . .'

He interrupted her, speaking in English since only an Anglo-Saxon could so molest a language. 'What is your name, please?'

'For God's sake, he's missing . . .'

'I do have to have your name, señora.'

'Rachael Cooper.'

'And you live where?'

'Ca'n Oliver. In the huerta.'

'When did you last see your husband?'

'Yesterday morning, when I went out to do some shopping.'

'What time was that?'

'About ten. When I got back, he wasn't here and his car was gone.'

'Were you expecting him to return last night?'

'Of course I was.'

'Have you spoken to friends to discover if he's with them?'

'No one's seen him. Something terrible's happened, I know it has.'

'Do you have reason to suppose he might be in trouble? Has he received any threats?'

'No.'

If the husband really had disappeared, then an investigation should start immediately. But ninety-nine times out of a hundred, 'missing' husbands preferred not to be found

45

until they had had time to concoct a story good enough to allay the suspicions of their wives. Added to which – though, of course, this was not in any sense a deciding factor – by the time he'd driven to the huerta, talked to the señora, and determined the facts, it would be long after lunch time. 'Señora, rest assured that almost all missing persons turn up sooner rather than later. But to make certain there is no obvious cause for concern, I'll be along as soon as I have finished some very important work which, regretfully, I cannot delay.' He said goodbye quickly – women when emotional could become very argumentative – and replaced the receiver. He settled back in the chair.

CHAPTER 7

Over the years, the slowly rising land of La Huerta de Llueso had been overtaken and overlaid by luxurious homes, gardens, swimming pools, and even hard tennis courts, so that now only a bare half of the area was under cultivation. It was a sad sight for anyone who could remember when every last centimetre of every field had been worked.

The narrow lane had been designed for mule carts, not cars. As Alvarez slowly approached a very sharp right-hand bend, made blind by the house on the corner, a Mercedes came round at speed and was forced to brake fiercely enough to make the tyres squeal shrilly. The driver sounded the horn and angrily waved at Alvarez to back. Alvarez did so until the road briefly widened sufficiently for two vehicles to pass. The Mercedes drew level. 'Pity you didn't ever learn to drive,' the man behind the wheel shouted in English through the opened window before accelerating away.

Alvarez thought up an answer after the Mercedes's dust had settled. He continued on around the corner, turned left a hundred metres on. Now he was level with a small orange grove in which a man was working with a Roman plough, pulled by a mule, a sight which in the past decade sadly had become rare. Alvarez braked the car to a halt, leaned across to lower the passenger window. 'Felipe.'

Caimari shouted at the mule, which came to a stop, head drooping. He dropped the reins, walked between orange trees, came to a stop, and looked up – at this point, the road was a metre higher than the field. 'It's you, Enrique! Not seen you for a long time.'

'Life gets even busier. How's the family?'

'Can't complain.'

He was of a generation who had endured great want and hardship and had learned the truth in the old Mallorquin saying, Do not complain that the rich man is robbing you lest he realize you still have something worth stealing. 'Which is Ca'n Oliver, owned by English people?'

He thought. 'Along the next dirt track to the right. The land belonged to old Serra until he died.'

'D'you know the English señor who lives there?'

'I've seen him. He's not seen me.'

Alvarez correctly understood that the Englishman was one of those foreigners who snobbishly ignored the locals. 'His wife says he's gone missing since yesterday morning.'

'Surprised she's bothered to report it.'

'Why d'you say that?'

'It don't mean nothing. And if you ain't anything better to do than talk, I have.' He turned, stumped his way back between the trees, picked up the reins, shouted at the mule and resumed ploughing.

Alvarez drove on until he reached a dirt track on his right, turned on to this. A couple of hundred metres on, a drive flanked by oleanders, grown as trees, not bushes, led up to a turning circle in front of a very large bungalow. Visible were flower beds which were a mass of colour, and part of a lawn that looked fit enough for bowling. Because the land sloped very gradually all the way to the distant shore, Llueso Bay was visible; seen at this distance, all development around the water became mere blotches that hardly diminished the beauty of the scene.

The door opened and he turned to face a young woman in neat maid's uniform. He introduced himself.

'You'd best come in instead of standing out there,' she said pertly.

He stepped into the large, air-conditioned hall, almost icily cool in comparison with the heat outside. 'Has there been any news of the señor?' she asked.

'I'm afraid not.'

'I do hope nothing terrible's happened.'

'I doubt it has . . . When did you last see him?'

'Yesterday morning.'

'Tell me about it.'

'Well, it was after the visitor had gone. I heard a noise of something falling here, in the hall, and came out to see what had happened. The señor had knocked the jug in which they keep pencils on to the floor.' She pointed to a small beautifully proportioned side table with fluted frieze and tapered legs, on which stood a heavily chased silver jug next to a telephone and answering unit. 'When I saw his face I thought he must be ill, but when I asked him if anything was wrong, he didn't seem to hear. Just went out and slammed the front door behind himself.'

'And then?'

'I picked up the pencils and the jug, put 'em on the table, went back to the kitchen to help Clara.'

'Did he drive off?'

'Don't expect the likes of him to walk, do you? Left as if the devil was tapping him on the shoulder. As I said to Clara, I'm glad I wasn't standing in front of the car.'

'Can you say why you thought he might be ill?'

'Not really . . . I mean, it's not easy to say. You look at someone and think he's not well, but it's difficult to explain exactly why you do. D'you understand?'

'Perfectly. He didn't say anything to you?'

'Not a word. It was like he didn't even know I was there.'

'Do you know who the visitor was?'

'Never seen him before.'

'When he was here, d'you think he and the señor might have been having a row?'

'When you're in the kitchen, you can't hear anything of what goes on in the sitting-room.'

'And the señora did not return until after the señor had left?'

'Quite a long time after.'

'She must have been surprised not to find him at home?'

'Can't rightly say.'

49

'Did you tell her you'd been worried that he might be ill?'

She shook her head. 'I didn't say nothing . . . The thing is, neither of 'em likes us saying what we think.'

'Then you had no reason to mention it,' he said reassuringly. 'I'd better have a word with the señora now.'

'Come on through with me. As far as I know, she's out by the pool, swimming or sunbathing.'

With or without a costume? he found himself wondering as he followed Rosa into the sitting-room. She suggested he waited there, leaving him no immediate chance to find out the answer to his question. She went out through the French windows on to the patio, in shade, thanks to the overhead roof, and disappeared from sight. He looked around himself. The furniture and furnishings spoke of money and taste. Chinese carpets, pelmeted curtains, luxuriously comfortable chairs and settee, occasional tables in a very dark, shiny wood, two glass-fronted display cabinets in which were some of the finer Lladro pieces, a bookcase filled with matching, leatherbound books, framed paintings of local scenes . . .

Movement, half seen, caught his attention and he turned. Through one window and then the French windows, he saw a woman approach across the patio. Words flooded his mind. Wavy blonde hair styled by a winsome zephyr; wide, deep blue eyes that could spur a cripple to run a kilometre merely to gain the favour of their rich glance; lips so shapely that Helen of Troy would pout with vexation; a body – enticingly, partially revealed as the lightweight swimming robe swirled to her movements – that undoubtedly could wear even the most mini of bikinis with nothing but credit . . . He halted the words, alarmed by their exuberance. No man was a greater fool than one for whom middle age was no longer a complete stranger, who looked at youth and thought himself young again . . .

She entered, closed the door, retied the belt of the swimming robe. 'Are you the person I spoke to this morning?'

'Yes, I am, señora.'

'It's taken you long enough to get here.'

She possessed the arrogance of youth as well as the arrogance of wealth. 'I'm sorry, but as I think I mentioned over the phone, I had to complete some very important work before I could come here.'

'My husband isn't important?'

'As I also mentioned, in almost all cases of the sudden disappearance of an adult, the person concerned has suffered no harm and soon gets in touch with someone to explain the reason for the disappearance.'

'I haven't heard from Oliver.'

'It is still relatively early and . . .'

'He'd know how terrified I'd be; he'd never let me suffer like this if he could help it.'

The question that formed in his mind was as inevitable as it was unwelcome. Would a woman very distressed by her husband's disappearance choose to spend her time by the swimming pool rather than searching everywhere for him?

'We're supposed to be flying to England tonight because the cruise starts tomorrow.'

'A cruise?'

'Oliver's always wanted to see the Arctic, though God knows why. When he saw the cruise advertised, he said we'd go on it even though it costs a small fortune. But if we don't fly tonight, we can't join the ship in time tomorrow.'

This directly contradicted the possibility that had begun to form in his mind only a moment before. He should have remembered that a person's reactions to any situation were often a poor guide to his emotions; where one would cry, another might appear quite calm . . . A rich man was always very careful of his money; he would never willingly forgo the enjoyment of something for which he had paid. 'Señora, I will need to ask many questions so perhaps we could sit?'

She crossed to the settee, sat. He settled on one of the

chairs. 'Have you spoken to everyone who might be able to help?'

'Of course I have.'

'And no one knows where your husband might be?'

'No. But it was all too obvious what some of them thought.'

'And what did they think?'

'Since malicious gossip is the favoured pastime, they decided he was with another woman.'

'I very much regret having to do this, but I must ask, is that possible?'

'You think he'd prefer one of those dried-up prunes to me?'

Crudely put, but who drank brackish water when champagne was on offer? 'I understand there was a visitor yesterday morning – was he a friend of your husband's?'

'Oliver had no idea who he was.'

'Are you sure of that?'

'When I told Oliver that a man called White had phoned and would be arriving at midday to see him, he was very annoyed because he thought the man must be selling something.'

'Did Señor White say where he is staying?'

'No. There was no way we could get back on to him or Oliver would have done so and told him not to bother to come. He was very American and just assumed he'd be welcome.'

'Can you be certain he is American?'

'You don't get an accent like that from anywhere else.'

'You weren't here when he arrived yesterday morning?'

'I was out shopping.'

He wondered why she'd suddenly spoken with unnecessary emphasis? 'Is there anything you can think of, señora, which might suggest why the meeting with Señor White so disturbed your husband?'

'Who's said it did?'

'Your maid told me that just before the señor left the

house, he looked so upset she thought he had been taken ill.'

'Neither of them has said anything to me. How can people be so stupid?'

'It wasn't stupidity. She came to the conclusion she must have been mistaken because had the señor been taken ill, he must surely have said so. And she didn't want needlessly to alarm you. But in the light of what has happened, it seems possible that the señor was not ill, he was concerned.'

'About what?'

'You know of nothing that might answer that question?'

'Haven't I said, I don't?'

Once again, that emphasis. Something was giving her sharp concern, yet she wasn't prepared to say what it was . . .

She suddenly stood, crossed to the French windows, and looked out. 'What can have happened to him?'

'At the moment, I fear I have absolutely no idea.'

She turned round. 'It has to be something awful or he'd be here, getting ready to leave to catch the plane tonight.'

'We must hope that he turns up in time.'

'And if he doesn't?'

'Then I fear that you will miss the cruise. I am sure that in the circumstances you will not wish to go on your own.'

'Of course not.'

For the third time she spoke in such a way as to attract his curiosity. Was she secretly hoping her husband would never return? That reminded him of what Caimari had said earlier . . . 'One last thing, señora. What kind of car does the señor drive and what is its registration number?'

'It's a BMW. But I don't know what the number is.'

'That doesn't matter. I can find out from the records.' He stood. 'I can assure you, señora, that I shall be doing everything possible to learn why your husband has disappeared.' A double-edged assurance if ever there had been one.

CHAPTER 8

Alvarez drove back to the field in which Caimari was working and parked in front of the bottom gate, leaving just enough room for another vehicle to pass. He climbed out of the car and stared at the scene, so drawn by the sights and sounds that for a while he was not conscious of the burning heat of the sun. Cicadas shrilled, starting and stopping as if to a conductor's baton; in the field beyond a rough line of prickly-pear cacti, a small flock of sheep were, with ridiculous optimism, grazing stubble, marking their progress with the unrhythmic, flat-toned clanging of the bells around their necks; a flock of pigeons rose, with clapping wings, from another field; the piping calls of unseen guinea-fowl suggested they were even more worried than usual; chained dogs whose job was to guard fields (though no one knew quite how a field could be stolen) barked in an intermittent but interminable chorus; a kestrel hovered, wings beating, tail swerving, then flew off in a curving sweep. Alvarez drew in several deep breaths and convinced himself that not only could he distinguish the pungent, bittersweet smell of the orange trees, but also the rich muskiness of the newly turned earth. His thoughts, ever susceptible to memories of his youth, soared into pretentious mode. Man's umbilical cord to true happiness was to be found in participation in the endless cycle of the soil. But modern life, which had taken so many men away from the soil, taught that happiness lay in amassing ever more, ever bigger riches and so men never understood their growing discontent . . .

He walked up the half-metre strip of unploughed headland that ran alongside the stone wall until he came level

54

with Caimari. The mule plodded towards him, head down, looking as if about to run out of all energy, yet continuing at the same even speed; drawing, as much from its own skills as Caimari's, a furrow almost as straight as an arrow.

Caimari brought the mule to a halt, released the reins. 'You ain't found anything to do yet?'

'I don't mind taking a turn to give you a break.'

'And smash my plough?'

'I can still draw a neat furrow.'

'When there's not a tree to run into.'

Alvarez took a pack of Celtas from his pocket. 'D'you smoke?'

Caimari took a cigarette. He had always been a small man; age was beginning to shorten him still further. Lines in his face formed a map of hardship and suffering, and the quiet cunning that had enabled him to overcome both.

Alvarez flicked open a lighter, held it out. 'How are the oranges looking?'

They both stared at the nearest trees, whose fruit could only just be distinguished. 'Could be better,' Caimari said.

Alvarez had not really expected any other answer. Only a farmer who was a fool allowed that his crops were good – the gods of drought, rain, wind, and pest, were always ready to punish optimism. 'I've been told Javier's giving up. Says he can't make money out of sheep any more, not with all the lamb coming from abroad that's in the shops cheaper than it costs to rear.'

Caimari snickered. 'He's giving up because he's taking so much money from the government he doesn't need to work any more.'

Alvarez was not surprised to hear that. It had not taken the local farmers long to discover that the Common Agricultural Policy was a horn of plenty – there were grants for more sheep than one owned, for buying tractors that were never delivered, for modernizing barns that didn't exist. 'What's he going to do with the land?'

'Leave it fallow. The only person willing to rent it was Virgilio and Javier wasn't having any of him!'

'Why not?'

'You can ask? You didn't know that his grandfather and Virgilio's came to blows?'

The rich mixture that was the peasant, Alvarez thought, proud to see himself as one. The traditionalist and the opportunist. The grandsons who prolonged a feud even though they'd probably no clear idea what it was about, who made a fortune out of bureaucrats so stupid they would pay others to do what had always been done.

They smoked, the air so still that the smoke hardly rippled until a metre above their heads.

'There's something I'd like to know,' Alvarez said.

Caimari's expression became blank.

'You told me earlier you were surprised Señora Cooper had bothered to report her husband was missing. Why?'

'How should I know why he's disappeared?'

'I'm asking why you're surprised?'

Caimari smoked. Alvarez waited, knowing that impatience would merely earn the other's amused contempt.

'Did you know Narcis Serra?' Caimari finally asked.

'To talk to, that's all.'

'Who'd want to do anything more when someone's daft enough to gamble away his land?' Caimari spoke with brief anger. To lose one's land through stupidity was the ultimate sin. 'His place was bought by a German who spent more pesetas than there are stars in the skies on a house and swimming pool. He wanted a huge garden and Jorge looked after it. When the German sold, Jorge stayed on.'

'Jorge?'

'Amoros. He talked to Eduardo and Eduardo talked to me. The señor was away and only the señora was there. Jorge went to fetch something he'd forgotten – more like to pinch some flowers to sell – and saw the señora in the swimming pool.'

'What was unusual about that?'

'She'd no costume on.'

'That must have cheered him up!'

56

Caimari sniggered. 'Not much he could do about it.'

'He's not that old.'

'Maybe he ain't, but the man in the pool with her was a lot younger.'

'Was he naked?'

'Would you keep your clothes on if she was flashing it around?'

So his intuition, imagination, call it what one would, had been correct.

Despite his best efforts, Alvarez could not find a reason for not phoning.

'Yes?' said the superior chief's secretary in her superior, plummy voice.

'May I speak to Señor Salas, please?' He was not surprised when she failed to offer him the politeness of asking him to wait. Her manners were a reflection of those of the superior chief.

As he waited, he stared through the window at the wall of the building on the opposite side of the road and tried not to imagine Rachael in the nude.

'What is it?'

Salas was a man of moods; bad tempered and very bad tempered. It sounded as if he were suffering the latter.

'Earlier today, señor, I received a report of a missing man and I have made a preliminary investigation. I judge there is cause . . .'

'Did you by any chance think to ascertain the name of the person?'

'Yes, of course, señor.'

'Regrettably, where you are concerned there can be no such certainty. What is it?'

'Cooper. He's an Englishman and . . .'

'With such a name, he is hardly likely to be a Spaniard. Who reported him missing?'

'His wife.'

'Why does she think he's missing?'

'Because he has not returned home and . . .'

57

'If a wife reports her husband is missing, do you find it strange that he has not returned home?'

'What I was about to add, señor, was that although there can be circumstances when a man's absence is explicable, in this case . . .'

'Circumstances such as what?'

'Perhaps a lady friend whose company he has enjoyed for an overlong period.'

'Alvarez, this is not the first time I've been forced to comment on the most regrettable urge you suffer, that of introducing a libidinous motif into a case.'

'I've only mentioned what is already there.'

'You know as fact, then, that Señor Cooper has a mistress?'

'No, señor, but . . .'

'Then why introduce the possibility unless it is because you derive a perverted pleasure from doing so?'

'It was you who introduced it, señor, not I.'

'How the devil do you mean?'

'Well, maybe not directly. But you had said that if a man was missing he could not have returned home and so I was trying to explain that circumstances might show that if he was missing from home, he wasn't missing despite his wife's belief that he was. If this were so . . .'

'I've had a very heavy day. Try not to increase its weight beyond all endurance. If such a thing is possible, tell me the facts simply and without any elaboration or explanation.'

Alvarez began to detail the brief course of his investigation. He was interrupted when he described how Amoros unexpectedly visited Ca'n Oliver and had seen Rachael and an unknown man swimming . . .

'Are you suggesting that there is any significance in that fact?'

'I think there has to be.'

'You really find it impossible to envisage that a married woman can invite a male friend for a swim without eagerly assuming she is indulging in an adulterous affair?'

'It is difficult when one knows that both were naked.'

There was a long pause. 'I would find my job considerably less wearing had you ever learned even the rudiments of logical reporting.'

There were no further interruptions.

'So I think,' Alvarez concluded, 'that we should ask Traffic to identify the registration number of the señor's car and then ask all patrols to keep an eye out for it. Remembering that he was due to fly from the island this evening in order to go on an expensive cruise, I think one must assume that he has suffered seriously, perhaps fatally.'

'Then I have no doubt that within the next forty-eight hours he will reappear, unharmed.' Salas cut the connection.

CHAPTER 9

'You're late,' Dolores snapped.

'I'm very sorry,' Alvarez replied humbly.

'The meal is probably ruined.'

'Never, with you doing the cooking.'

'Only a man could say something so foolish.' But the implied compliment was sufficient to prevent any further complaints. She returned into the kitchen.

Alvarez sat at the dining-table, picked up one of the tumblers. 'Shove the coñac over.'

Jaime turned sideways to look at the kitchen doorway.

Alvarez leaned across and picked up the bottle. 'Is this all that's left?' he asked, as he stared at the few centimetres of brandy.

Jaime turned back, reached under the table and brought up a second bottle of Soberano, three parts full.

'What the hell's going on?'

'She's on again about drinking.' He jerked his head in the direction of the kitchen. 'Watching television and some bloody fool doctor says that half the family problems are caused by people who drink. Doesn't add that the other half are caused by people who don't drink. That's started a donkey galloping about in her brain. Told me that from now on I'm not having more than one drink before a meal. So I leave the nearly empty bottle on the table and every time she looks in to see what's what, there's the same amount left.' He winked. 'There's always a way if you're smart enough to find it,' he said boastfully.

Alvarez poured himself a large brandy, passed the bottle back. Jaime hid it under the table.

'Have you really been busy or was that just to shut her up?' Jaime asked, as he straightened up.

'A husband's gone missing and I've been trying to find out what's happened to him.'

'A foreigner, I suppose? None of us would ever get away with it.'

Alvarez dropped three ice cubes into the tumbler. 'A rich Englishman.'

'Then he's found himself someone young and willing and forgotten how time flies when one's enjoying oneself.'

'With a wife like his, that seems unlikely.'

'What's so special about her?'

'Ever imagined yourself in a Ferrari?'

Jaime, his perplexity obvious, stared at him. 'What's that got to do with anything?'

'How d'you feel when you realize you'll never drive around in anything but a Fiesta?'

'You've not been working late, you've been drinking early.'

'She's the woman of your dreams.'

'You don't know my dreams.'

'Swims in the nude.'

'You're telling me you've seen her?'

'Jorge Amoros, who does their garden, has.'

Jaime shed his air of sophisticated indifference. 'What's he ever done to be so bloody lucky?' he said bitterly.

Alvarez had not been sufficiently long in the office to prepare himself for work when the phone rang. The green BMW owned by Señor Cooper had been found two kilometres west of Contaix, at a point where the coast road ran within metres of the cliff face. The car had been searched. On the front passenger seat was a copy of *The Times*, open at page four. One of the two men in the patrol car was reasonably fluent in English and he said that the article in the middle of the page reported the suicide of a businessman who had thrown himself off a cliff in Wales after learning that his small engineering company had been

61

bankrupted by the fraudulent actions of a trusted employee. In the glove box was a gold signet ring and a wallet containing just over forty thousand pesetas in notes, several credit cards, and an English driving licence. In the rear well was an empty bottle of Teacher's Highland Cream whisky and three exhausted foil strips, of the kind used to hold medicinal pills.

The sea came right up to the cliff face and there would only be traces of his having fallen if he had done so in too shallow an arc and struck the rock face during his descent; even then, it might be virtually impossible to detect these.

What action was to be taken? He said the car was to be kept under guard until he had examined it.

After the call was over, he settled back in the chair. Contaix was on the north coast, at a point where the jagged, stark cliffs were a hundred, or more, metres high. When oar or sail had been the only form of marine propulsion, ships had frequently been driven ashore by adverse winds, with the usual result that whole crews had been drowned. There were villagers who claimed that in a gale from the north, the cries of drowning men could clearly be heard above the howling wind. Because the village had once been all but isolated, the inhabitants were much more inward looking than most – it was said that they would always greet a stranger with a scowl rather than a smile and there was the expression, as bloody-minded as a Contaixian. It was a village, indeed an area, that he hardly knew, not so much because of the nature of the inhabitants, but because it was a land of heights and depths and both these terrified him.

The drive to Contaix was one that would have confounded all those tourists who believed the island to consist of nothing but beaches, happy hours, lager louts, and concrete. The road wound its way up and down and around mountain after mountain, some bare rock, some covered with pine trees. Sometimes it seemed as if the walls of rock were about to fall and crush, sometimes there were distant views of great natural beauty. In a valley there would be a small village and cultivated land, beyond would be a wild fastness in which only the road itself gave evidence of human intervention.

He passed through Contaix – untouched by tourism because it was seldom visited; a jig-saw of roads, mostly very narrow, lined by shuttered, stone-built houses with bleak exteriors – and a cutting that had had to be blasted out, to reach a short stretch of narrow, relatively flat land, halfway along which was a signposted viewing area which lay between the road and the cliff. The green BMW and a Guardia Renault were parked in the centre of the area. He turned off the road and braked to a halt behind the Renault, climbed out. Llueso had been swelteringly hot; here, it was merely pleasantly warm, thanks to the sea breeze.

The driver of the Renault spoke through the opened window. 'It's taken you long enough to get here.'

'I'm a busy man.'

'So are we, but we've had to sit here and watch the seagulls.'

'You must know old Marx's motto – each according to his abilities. Anything more turned up?'

'No.'

'I'll check out the car, then.'

'Tell you one thing. In this day and age, it's a miracle that a car like that can be left standing around and not be stripped out.'

Alvarez went forward to the BMW and searched it, surprised to discover that everything was as had been reported – the newspaper on the front passenger seat, the signet ring and wallet in the glove locker, the empty bottle of whisky and three silver-foil strips in the back well. In addition, three cigarette stubs were in the front ashtray and in the boot was an empty, scrumpled pack of Lucky Strike.

He crossed to the recently erected Armco barrier – in the past, people had been left to decide how stupid they were – and with each step his fear grew. It was ridiculous and he always despised himself because of it; again and again,

63

he'd promised himself that he would overcome it; but now he knew once more the terror that made him want to turn and run, the siren's song that tried to lure him on by turning his terrible fear into a terrible longing . . . He reached the Armco and leaned against it, sweating, his stomach churning. Before him was a dramatic scene of sudden, soaring depth and a deep blue sea, but he would rather have faced a king cobra. His torment was not yet at an end. Summoning his last reserve of inner strength, he leaned forward until he could look down the face of the cliff. Below – kilometres below – the sea washed against the rock to cause brief ripples of white foam. If a man . . . He tightened his grip still further . . . If a man fell accidentally, there had to be the possibility that on the way down he would slam into the cliff face; if he jumped, he would probably fall in a curve that would keep him clear of that. In the latter case, would the impact with the water knock him unconscious? Were there rocks just below the surface? If he retained consciousness and tried desperately to escape that which he had just courted, was it reasonable to accept that he could have swum along the coast until he found somewhere to land? All questions that might need answering. All questions that he was not going to answer because there was nothing on this earth that would persuade him to descend on a rope to search the cliff face for signs of contact . . .

He released his grip, turned, and walked slowly because the two cabos were watching him. He came to a stop by the driving door of the Renault.

The driver stared up at him, squinting because of the sun. 'Are you all right?'

'Why d'you ask?'

'Because you look bloody awful; like you died yesterday.'

'Then you can start showing some respect for the dead. Was the BMW locked?'

'Yeah, and no sign of the key. But there are brains in

64

our outfit, so we got in touch with the distributors and they provided another key.'

'Where's that now?'

The second cabo slapped the breast pocket of his grey-green shirt.

'OK. You drive the car into Palma and leave it with Traffic for a detailed examination.'

'I'm finished and off home in an hour.'

'For the good officer,' Alvarez said with hypocritical satisfaction, 'duty always comes before pleasure.'

CHAPTER 10

When Alvarez drove up to Ca'n Oliver, a battered grey Seat 127 was parked in the turning circle. He climbed out of the Ibiza, crossed to the front door, rang the bell.

Rosa opened the door. 'Is there any news?'

He prevaricated. 'Nothing definite.'

'I couldn't sleep properly last night, thinking of what could have happened to him.'

That, he was certain, had not been said for effect. It was in the Mallorquin character to be concerned by another's misfortune, even when there was little enough reason to like that person. 'I've come to have a word with the señora.'

'Then you're out of luck. She left here after breakfast and hasn't been back.'

Conducting her own search? Or . . . ?

'Did she tell you how to get hold of her if that was necessary?'

'No.'

If searching, wouldn't she have done so?

'But maybe Señor Field knows where she is.'

'Is he the owner of the Seat outside?'

'That's right. He's a friend of the family.'

'Then I'll have a word with him.'

As he entered the hall, she said: 'Last time I saw him, he was in the sitting-room. You know the way.'

He was amused that she was not going to be bothered to announce him. When the shepherd was out of sight, the sheep strayed. In any case, no Mallorquin saw merit in unnecessary formality.

He entered the sitting-room to see an elderly man by the French windows. 'Señor Field?'

'That's right,' Field answered in Castilian. 'And you are?'

It was very unusual to meet an Englishman who not only chose to speak Castilian, but did so with a degree of fluency. 'Inspector Alvarez, Cuerpo General de Policia.'

'Good morning, Inspector,' Field said with risible formality.

Batwing ears, a hairline that was receding asymmetrically, bushy eyebrows, slightly lopsided mouth, and a very pointed jaw, combined to suggest to Alvarez that he was speaking to a man who could see the humour in life because he had experienced the pain. 'I hoped to speak to Señora Cooper, but Rosa tells me she is not here. Have you any idea where she might be?'

'None at all.'

'Or when she'll be back?'

'Not really, except obviously . . . At least, I'm sure . . . I'm not making any sense, am I? But I was so surprised and upset to learn what's happened . . . Won't you sit down and I'll try to explain a little more rationally.' Once they were both seated, Field continued: 'I'm an old friend; known Oliver for more years than I care to remember. So when they go away, which they do quite often, he gets me to come round and check that everything's running smoothly.' He hesitated, then added: 'Oliver finds it difficult to accept that the staff are more than capable. So when I turned up here this morning, I expected them to be in London or aboard the ship . . . I suppose Rachael has gone out to ask anyone and everyone if they've seen Oliver . . . Have you any news?'

'The señor's car has been found on the north coast. There is no sign of him and I'm afraid it seems possible because of the circumstances that he may have committed suicide by throwing himself over the cliff.'

'Ridiculous!'

'Why do you say that?'

Field was embarrassed. 'I . . . I'm sorry, I didn't mean to

be rude. It's just that the idea is impossible because if ever he wanted to commit suicide, throwing himself off a cliff is the one way he would never choose, however desperate.'

'Can you be quite so certain?'

'Positive. He's terrified of heights. Even a staircase around an open well makes him hug the wall side. I don't suppose you find it easy to understand?'

'On the contrary. Regrettably, I also suffer from alto-phobia.'

'That's very bad luck . . . Jumping over a cliff is some-thing he just couldn't do.'

'Probably not. But I do wonder if there is not the possibil-ity that since a person's mind surely has to be very upset to contemplate suicide, might he not choose the method which he fears most to render the act even more traumatic for both himself and others?'

'You lose me on that one! All I can say is, the last time I saw him, his mind seemed as clear as ever.'

'And that was when?'

'Saturday afternoon.'

'Since you are an old friend of the señor's, I suppose you know him very well?'

'Probably as well as one person can know another.'

'Would you say he is happy living on the island?'

'Far happier than in England.'

'Why is that?'

'The climate, the people, the way of life.'

'What particular aspect of the way of life so appeals to him?'

'Well, the fact that . . .' He came to a stop.

'Yes, señor?'

'It's going to be difficult to explain without sounding rather disloyal.'

'I need your help in order to try to understand what kind of a person Señor Cooper is because if I can learn that, I may be able more accurately to understand what has happened to him. What you tell me may enable me to recognize as important something I would otherwise dismiss as unimportant. That is not disloyalty.'

Field rubbed his chin with thumb and forefinger, trying to make up his mind. He looked up, and directly at Alvarez. 'If I'm to explain things, it'll be something of a long story.'

'We have the saying, Time is made for man, not man for time.'

'Which explains why most people here live to a ripe old age . . . I first met Oliver through carrying out work for him – I'm a picture restorer, or rather, was before I retired. That was soon after he'd married Davina. It was never the happiest of marriages; she had no natural interest in art and couldn't be bothered to develop any, and so didn't appreciate his success in his chosen sector of the art world, while he had little or no sympathy for her social aspirations. It was her money that started the gallery and bought the house and she'd determined where they lived – with typical misjudgement, in the heart of senile suburbia. She blamed him when they remained outsiders. But there was never any chance it could be otherwise. He hadn't been to a good school and was making a success of life despite his background. He was clever and he was in art. Added to which, Davina's money was new money and she wasn't the kind of person to hide that fact successfully.

'Ironically, his professional life which should have been so very much happier than his social one, wasn't. I've told Oliver more than once that his biggest problem was not that he was right, but that he made other people aware that they were wrong. Soon after he bought the gallery, he publicly and unsubtly doubted the attribution of a painting which had recently been authenticated by a couple of the best known experts. That he was proved right naturally increased the resentment of the two and as they carried a great deal of influence, they made certain he was never received into the art world's establishment. He had been proved absolutely justified in his championing of Poperen, but because of enmity and jealousy, it took years longer than it should have done to establish that fact.'

69

'Then it was his unhappiness in both his marriage and his work that brought him to this island?'

'Yes and no. The recession hit the art world hard and it looked as if the gallery would be forced to close. But then he managed to sell two Poperens privately for record prices and finances looked considerably healthier. That's when Davina died.

'Rachael had been working for him and it wasn't long after Davina's death before he told me he was marrying her. Frankly, I congratulated him, thinking that he was making as big a mistake as when he married Davina – he was still shocked and she was only half his age. Which proves that friends' judgements should always be ignored. She persuaded him to leave England and come out here to live and that turned out to be the best thing he could have done. The expatriates' community is not a very large one, but it is widely based, most people take the trouble to get on with their fellows, and there are a surprising number who are ready to go to a lot of trouble to help others. Of course, since most are English, society is stratified – we may have invented the theory of democracy, but the practice always panics us. One stratum is defined solely by money – if you're rich, you're in, however stupid or boring you are. Oliver was wealthy enough to qualify and the fact that he was highly intelligent in artistic matters was not held against him. Having bought an expensive house and car, he was received into the full social whirl.'

'So the señor's second marriage has been a happy one?'

'It has.'

'There have been no problems?'

'Why should there be?'

'It is an unfortunate fact that when a husband is considerably older than his wife, she sometimes seeks a companion of her own age.'

'There's been nothing like that.'

Field had spoken with such emphasis that Alvarez gained the impression he had been denying the possibility to himself as much as to his listener. 'You are a loyal friend.'

'I have every reason to be. When my wife was so ill, Oliver went out of his way to help me. One does not forget that sort of thing.'

There was, Alvarez thought, no doubting the sincerity with which Field had spoken.

'There's something more. Oliver gave, and gives, me the confidence I need to continue painting on my own account. Mary used to encourage me and say my work possessed a special quality, but I was sufficient of a realist to know that wives don't make the truest critics. But then Davina and Oliver came to our place for a meal and Mary insisted on showing them my latest painting. He didn't comment at the time and I presumed this was a silence of politeness, but later he said he'd been intrigued by a sense of quality and thought I had real potential and would I like him to help me in so far as he could? A question that didn't have to be asked twice! Since then, he's done everything he can to help, which potentially adds up to a lot because he still has contact with important people in the art world.'

'And you are now successful?'

'Shall we say, I'm improving. But Rembrandt isn't ever going to have to move over.'

'I wish you every success, señor ... Tell me, have you recently heard the name Señor White; he is probably either an American or a Canadian?'

Field thought for a while, then shook his head. 'The name doesn't ring any bells.'

'He visited the señor here on Sunday morning, which raises the possibility that something happened between them which caused the señor to leave the house unexpectedly. I need to meet Señor White and ask him if that is indeed the case, but until I can identify him, it is impossible.'

'Can't Rachael help you?'

'She does not know who he is or why he visited the señor and she was not at home at the time.'

'What about Rosa or Clara?'

'Unfortunately, they cannot help.'

'Very frustrating!'

'A common problem!' He stood. 'Thank you for being so frank.'

'I hope I haven't given you an unflattering picture? If I have, that's wrong. Oliver has his faults, but who hasn't? And it's not given to many to have the inherent ability, taste, and confidence, to recognize and then promote a great artist in the face of indifference or ignorant hostility.'

'You are referring to the person you mentioned earlier?'

'Poperen used to be no more than a footnote to any article about the neo-impressionists; now he's in the main text, thanks entirely to Oliver.'

'Then indeed the señor is to be congratulated. But,' Alvarez added lightly, 'he would find my congratulations of small account since I know as little about art and artists as financiers and their mysteries. I have heard of the impressionists, of course, every time a painting is sold for more pesetas than a full ticket in El Gordo wins. But neo-impressionists? Are they a modern and unwelcome copy?'

'Not quite, though there are critics who'd appear to approve of that definition.' Enthusiasm for the subject spurred Field into speaking more quickly. 'Theirs was the theory of optical mixtures – that one obtains brighter and truer secondary colours by making a series of dots of primary colours which at a certain distance mix in an onlooker's eyes. Seurat and Pissarro are the best-known exponents.

'Poperen was dismissed by the critics long after these artists and others had become valued. They called his work too strict and formal, too controlled to have any meaning-ful relationship with the fleeting effects and momentary forms that good work had. Of course, that was all tosh. What really upset them was the fact that Poperen, who pursued vice vigorously – he died at thirty-seven from the combined effects of syphilis and alcohol – did not separate his paintings from his vice.'

'His paintings are obscene?'

'Not at first glance. Indeed, one can only appreciate their

obscenity by going right up to the painting which, of course, destroys the ethos of the theory. And further to confuse and annoy the critics, he gave his paintings titles that seemed to have no relevance – that was, unless and until one realized that these were a play on words and referred not to the main subjects, but to the "hidden" ones. The critics took all this as insults aimed directly and perversely at them. They were probably right . . . Does all that make sense?'

'As I said, I'm afraid I know so little about art that . . .' Alvarez became silent.

'In other words, it sounds like arrant nonsense? . . . I tell you what. Come and look at two of the paintings and you'll understand.'

Alvarez was supremely uninterested in the artistic feuds of dead artists, but Field's enthusiasm was such that he thought it would be churlish to say so. 'That would be very interesting.'

They went through into another room, half the size of the one they'd just left, which was both library and television room. On the wall facing the window hung two large paintings, in heavy, elaborate frames, above which were exhibition strip lights.

'Viewing distance is critical, so you start by standing there.'

Alvarez moved to where Field had indicated. The right-hand painting showed a river, filled with reflections, its banks spotted with flowers, that wound round to disappear from sight; a woman paddled at the edge of the water, where the bank was very low, and although her features were undefined, the viewer gained the impression that she was young, pretty, and romantically in love.

'Now move to your left. Keep the same distance away.'

In the second painting, a woman, again undefined yet unmistakably pretty, lay on a blanket on which was an unpacked hamper, in the centre of a field; beyond the field there was a wood; the sky, though clear overhead, promised stormy weather and by some alchemy of art,

73

this raised in the viewer's mind the impression that the woman's lover, out of sight, was in some danger of which she had no immediate knowledge, but would soon learn.

'Can you read the titles from there?'

'I think so. *The Cherry Biscuit.*'

'And the right-hand one?'

He moved across. '*Come Here.*'

'What do you make of those titles?'

'They appear to have nothing to do with the paintings.'

'"As meaningless as the work they should describe," was one critic's comment. And what offended him even more, since he was French, was that Poperen should use English titles . . . Now get as close as possible and look at the corners of the paintings.'

He moved forward. The picture came out of focus, blurred, resolved into a myriad of dots which ceased to have any coherence. At this point, he first discerned figures in the top corners. Yet only when even closer, could he make them out. A naked man and woman were engaged in a popular variation of a well-known enjoyment. That such detail and sense of passion could be painted into such minute figures ironically left him far more conscious of the artist's genius than did the compositions as a whole. He studied the figures in the left-hand corner – same variation, different position.

'Now does the title make sense?'

Come Here. Field had said that it referred to the 'hidden' composition. But it seemed not only an unnecessary exhortation, but also one that neither of the figures would at that moment be able to make.

'Poperen had a Spanish father and an English mother, from whom he probably inherited his love of playing with words.'

After a while, Alvarez said: 'I'm afraid I have a very slow brain.'

'Certainly no slower than all the critics who prided themselves on the brilliance of their intellects. It took an Englishman with a wide knowledge of Spanish slang to solve the riddle.'

That provided him with the solution. He laughed.

He moved to the left-hand painting. In the two bottom corners was the figure of a naked woman in a generous pose. *Cherry Biscuit.* Now that he knew there would be a double word play, he quickly understood.

'His sense of humour has been described as third-form smut,' Field said. 'I think that that is being rather harsh.'

'These paintings must be very valuable?'

Field jiggled some coins in the pockets of his linen trousers. 'The last major Poperens sold in London for a shade under four hundred thousand pounds. It's probable that with the market indicating recovery, that figure will soon be overtaken.'

Alvarez said, in somewhat awed tones: 'Then there is nine hundred thousand pounds, or more, on the wall?'

'I suppose the most generous estimate of their true value would be a hundred pounds each.'

'But you said . . . I don't understand.'

'I was quoting the value of the genuine article. These two paintings are fakes, forgeries, or copies, depending on your definitions, and their only value is in their frames which are somewhat elaborate for modern tastes. Oliver has a love for Poperen's work that equals a miser's lust for gold; but he couldn't afford to have even one of his minor paintings, having championed the artist so successfully. I'd done a fair amount of restoration work on Poperen's paintings – particularly on one that was badly damaged – and Oliver, defying the purists who claim that a true connoisseur can never enjoy what's false, asked me to see if I could make a reasonable copy of *The Cherry Biscuit*. He liked the result sufficiently to get me to do *Come Here* as well.'

'You painted the figures in the corners?'

'I did.'

'But they are incredible!'

'Only when you haven't seen the genuine article.'

Alvarez noted the touch of bitterness in Field's voice. It seemed misplaced. Perhaps they were not as miraculously painted as the originals, but to an amateur they were the work of genius. 'No wonder that Señor Cooper has had faith in your painting!'

Field's earlier diffidence suddenly returned. 'There is an ocean of difference between following in another's footsteps and leading the way ... Yet when I become depressed, Oliver cheers me up by saying that I can become a leader. I hope he's right.'

'I'm sure he has to be. Is there a painting of yours in this house for me to see?'

'I gave Oliver one, but I'm not certain where he's hung it and I don't like to look around; a bit too much like prying.'

'That's very understandable, so perhaps another time ... Señor, may I ask you to do me a favour? Since you are an old friend, I feel it would be better if you, rather than I, explain to the señora that her husband's car has been found, but that there is still no sign of him.'

'Of course,' Field said.

CHAPTER 11

The phone began to ring as Alvarez poured himself another drink. He passed the bottle to Jaime, who hid it under the table.

'Is anyone going to answer the phone?' Dolores demanded from the doorway of the kitchen.

They were surprised by the question.

'If you were paid to be idle, you'd be rich men.' She marched past them and through to the front room.

'If I could get my hands on that stupid old cow on television who said a loving husband would give a hand around the house, I'd tell her what I thought!' Jaime drank.

She returned. 'It's for you, Enrique.' Her voice sharpened. 'She says her name is Rosa. She sounds very young.'

'Rosa Puta. She's twelve and owns six fincas and three luxury flats along the Paseo Maritimo.'

She held her head a little higher and her mouth a little tighter as she continued through to the kitchen.

'You shouldn't have said that,' Jaime muttered.

'Only a joke,' Alvarez said, as he stood.

'But you know what she thinks of your jokes.'

He picked up his glass and went through to the front room. For once, Jaime was probably right. Never bait a fighting bull, stroke a spitting serpent, or jest with a virtuous woman. He lifted the receiver.

'It's me, Rosa, from Ca'n Oliver. I phoned the post and they gave me your number. I thought you'd want to know that Señor White has been here.'

'What did he want?'

'To speak to Señor Cooper.'

77

'He didn't know the señor had disappeared?'

'He wouldn't have called if he had, would he?'

He realized that because his thoughts had raced ahead of his tongue, he had sounded stupid. 'Was he surprised to hear that the señor was missing?'

'If you ask me, he was more like angry. Kept asking questions. I told him, I didn't know anything more than I'd said. So he left.'

'I don't suppose he gave any indication where he's staying?'

'Nothing like that. But knowing you was interested, I took the number of his car.'

He was so surprised by this display of initiative, that he said: 'I could kiss you for that.'

'Then it's a good job I didn't get his address as well!'

She gave him the registration number. The last two letters, CA, showed the car to be almost new. Remembering that White was a foreign visitor, the odds had to be that it was hired. He thanked her, said goodbye.

He drained his glass. The obvious conclusion was that since White had not known Cooper was missing, he could not have had a hand in the other's disappearance. But a clever man might reckon that to put a hand in a hornets' nest would suggest to others that he had not known it was one. And even if White's surprise, or anger, had been genuine and he had not known that Cooper was missing, he could in all probability explain why he had vanished ... About to ring Traffic in Palma to ask them to trace the number, he heard sounds that made it clear luncheon was being served. He went through to the dining-room and sat, filled his tumbler with wine. 'Where are the children?'

Jaime said, 'They're out to lunch.'

'Who with?'

He shrugged his shoulders.

'They are at Cecilia's,' Dolores snapped as she handed a bowl to Alvarez. 'Which is a very great mercy since they have not been shamed by hearing their uncle engage in an obscene conversation.'

78

About to put the spoonful of Pancuit into his mouth, Alvarez stared at her with confused surprise. 'Hear me doing what?' Some of the bread and garlic soup spilled back into the bowl and he hastily put the spoon into his mouth.

She served herself, sat.

'You can't think that Rosa is . . .'

She interrupted him. 'Being a respectable woman, I am not prepared to suggest what I thought when I heard my cousin say he wished to kiss a woman he himself described in a way I shall not repeat.'

The inference was so ridiculous that he forgot the wise words about jesting with a virtuous woman. 'Surely, being so respectable, they could only be respectable thoughts?'

She looked at him with her dark-brown eyes flashing. 'I have a headache,' she announced.

Jaime groaned.

A siesta was like a dream about paradise – when it was over, one longed to return but could not. It was twenty minutes later, during which time he'd enjoyed two cups of hot chocolate and two slices of coca, that Alvarez felt ready for work.

He drove through the narrow, winding roads of the village, intending to park in the old square, only to find that this was closed to traffic because workmen were preparing it for the festival. He swore.

Every side street seemed filled with cars, but eventually he found an empty parking spot by the health centre, only to lose it to a tourist. He swore again. Ten minutes later, he was forced to park on the outskirts, which left him with a long walk to the post, a prospect that left him too exhausted to swear yet again.

Breathless, sweating heavily, he slumped down in the chair in his office. He must, he finally accepted, give up smoking, reduce his drinking, and take up regular exercise.

He phoned Traffic. Would they trace the ownership of the car number he was about to give them . . .

He was interrupted. It had very recently been decreed that all such requests had to be made on the appropriate form and be countersigned by a superior officer. Forms were available only from Palma. Perhaps it would mean delay, but rules were rules . . . In turn, he interrupted. The identity of the car's owner was urgently needed in order to pursue an important investigation and the superior chief, who was a Madrileño and therefore extremely short tempered, had declared that he would personally have the cojones of anyone who delayed the investigation . . .

'Ring back in an hour's time,' snapped the other, annoyed to find himself outflanked.

Alvarez replaced the receiver, leaned back in the chair. White had to offer the most promising lead, but this could not be followed up for the moment. So what was the identity of the man who had swum naked with the señora?

Such heat as the island was now suffering sapped a man of all energy. His eyelids closed . . .

He left the post and walked across the square, now almost completely criss-crossed by white streamers, and up past the church. Slowing as the ground rose, he reached Carrer Almas, in the oldest part of the town. Outside the first house, an old couple were sitting in the shadows, enjoying the opportunity of conversing with passers-by as much as searching for a cooler freshness than they could find indoors. He chatted with them for a while, as custom dictated, before asking in which house Jorge Amoros lived. They directed him to one at the end of the road.

He stepped through the bead curtain into the front room, furnished to receive visitors, and called out. After a moment, Teresa came through from inside. She studied him briefly and said, her voice muffled because she did not have her teeth in her mouth: 'You're Enrique, Dolores's cousin.'

'That's right.'

'I saw her last week and she said . . .'

He listened patiently. For people of Teresa's generation,

gossip, not television, was the staff of life. Eventually, however, he had the chance to ask her where Jorge was. 'In the Bar Iberia,' she answered, surprised he should need to ask.

Amoros was seated at the far table in the bar, talking to a man whom Alvarez recognized, yet could not immediately identify. He ordered a brandy, paid, said to the owner: 'Who's that with Jorge? Know the face, but can't place the name.'

'Eduardo Serra.'

'Of course! His brother was Narcis.'

'That silly sod!' was the other's sour comment.

Alvarez carried his glass across to the table. Amoros and Serra stared up at him with the blank, mindless expression with which they would face any situation until they had judged it. 'Have you time for a word?' he said.

They hesitated. 'With me?' Serra finally asked.

'With Jorge.'

Amoros drained his glass. 'What d'you want?' he demanded with the antagonism towards authority, common to most islanders, that he could now express without fear of the consequences.

'To hear about life at Ca'n Oliver.'

Serra stood. 'The señor's still missing, then? Bloody good riddance.' He eased his way out from the table and left, not bothering to say goodbye.

Alvarez sat. 'What's made him more bitter than an unripe persimmon?'

Amoros peered into his glass.

'How about another?'

He pushed his glass across. 'And tell that bastard behind the bar to pour a proper sized coñac this time.'

Alvarez went to the bar, returned, passed a glass across, sat. 'I've been up at Ca'n Oliver a couple of times. There can't be a better garden this side of Palma and maybe not the other side, either.'

The praise had the desired effect. Amoros's initial antagonism melted, its final disappearance helped along by

81

another brandy. Alvarez brought Serra back into the conversation.

''Course, he doesn't like the señor.'

'Wouldn't have thought he'd have much to do with him.'

'Call yourself a detective? Don't know much about anything, do you? When the father died, the land was left to the two of 'em. Narcis, being a stupid bastard, gambled his half away and a German bought the land and had a palace built. All the time the building was going on there was no garden, so there wasn't any need for water apart from mixing the cement and concrete. Eduardo diverted the German's share down his channel. After the house was finished, he forgot to change things.' Amoros sniggered.

'And when the owner moved in?'

'He was a German, so money meant nothing. When there was no water arriving, he told me to buy. Three lorryloads a week at this time of the summer; fifteen thousand pesetas and he never worried! When God made foreigners, he made 'em dafter'n women.'

'Then Eduardo continued to enjoy all the water?'

'And went around boasting how smart he was and how he grew the best fruit and vegetables on the island. Everyone knew it was only because of the extra water. Then the German sold the house and the Englishman bought it.'

'Things changed?'

Amoros studied his empty glass. Alvarez took it and his own to the bar and had them refilled.

'The English señor is different. Rich, but if he'd a flock of sheep, he'd go round plucking the wool off the brambles to make certain he didn't lose a strand. Like when I plant out bulbs, he counts how many come up to see none have gone missing. Came up one day and asked why I was buying water when the land was entitled to it from the aqueduct. I tried to explain things, but he's difficult. Called in some smart abogado from Palma who said the land was entitled to the water and if Eduardo didn't stop pinching it, he'd find himself in court. 'Course, Eduardo said I was to tell the señor I was switching the water, but to continue to let it run through to his estanque. But the señor's such a suspicious bastard, he checked up and when he found it wasn't running, made me alter the baffles . . . So now most times Eduardo only gets the water that's rightly his. People are laughing.'

Only a peasant, Alvarez thought, could fully appreciate the measure of humiliation Serra would be suffering. To be outwitted by a foreigner was bad enough; to be jeered at by his fellows was worse. His sense of bitter, angry resentment might well have reached the point where the need to gain revenge far outstripped all sense of proportion or logic. Unexpectedly, a new possibility had opened up . . . Alvarez changed the subject. 'I met Señora Cooper yesterday. She's very lovely.'

'If you like 'em like that.'

'You're dead if you don't. I heard she's a bit of a handful?'

'The likes of you won't never get the chance to find out.'

'But some lucky lad did one Sunday?'

'If he didn't, he must be slower than a blind mule.'

'What exactly did you see?'

'She was showing her tits. Then she climbed out of the pool and showed all the rest.'

'And?'

'She and the bloke lay down on towels and sunbathed.'

'Have you any idea who he is?'

'Can't name him, but I've seen him around.'

'Where?'

'Down in the port, working on boats.'

'Did you mention what you saw to the señor?'

'Take me for that much of a bloody fool? He'd have asked her if it was true and she'd have said I was a dirty-minded liar and he'd have believed her, not me, because it's her what's got him by the short and curlies. I'd have been sacked. In any case, what them lot get up to, doesn't concern me.'

'I reckon that's fair enough.' Alvarez drained his glass.

'D'you know what's happened to the señor?'

'Right now, it looks like he may have committed suicide.'

'Why'd he want to be that daft?'

'That's what I'm trying to find out. D'you think he could have discovered the señora was planting horns on his head?'

'He's the great hidalgo. His kind take out their troubles on someone else, not themselves. Maybe his disappearing is something to do with the other man?'

'What other man?'

'The one what was watching the house through binoculars.'

'How long ago?'

'Something short of a week.'

'You saw him?'

'Wouldn't know about him if I hadn't, would I?'

'What did you do?'

'Didn't do nothing. He saw me looking at him and started moving the binoculars around as if he was one of those barmy foreigners what spend their time looking at birds. Like the one what asked me if I'd seen a black vulture recently and I told him I'd seen four that very afternoon.' Amoros stared into the past. 'That cheered him up so much he gave me a couple of coñacs from a bottle in his rucksack. If I'd've known four vultures would have got him that excited, I'd have made it a dozen.'

'Perhaps this man you saw really was looking for birds?'

'Until he saw me, he was looking at the house.'

'Can you describe him?'

'Taller than you and not nearly so fat.'

'I am not fat,' Alvarez said sharply. 'What about colour of hair and eyes, shape of ears and nose?'

'He was wearing some kind of a hat with a wide brim, and so what with the binoculars up to his eyes as well, I couldn't see nothing but the scar.'

'Where was that?'

'On his cheek.'

'Right or left?'

Amoros intently studied his empty glass.

Alvarez decided that it was not worth the cost of another brandy to discover that Amoros probably couldn't remember on which cheek the scar was.

He phoned Traffic from the office.

'The car's owned by Garaje Xima, in Cala Xima. And there's a message from my jefe. The next time you submit the request on the proper form, countersigned, or you won't get the information.'

Alvarez settled back in the chair. Cala Xima. A place to be avoided whenever possible.

He looked at his watch. Dolores would have started cooking supper. Small point, then, in starting anything fresh.

CHAPTER 12

In the brilliant sunshine, the bay was at its most beautiful, the water a dramatic blue, the mountains looking benign. It was Alvarez's hope that when St Peter opened the gates and he walked through, he would find himself on the shores of Llueso Bay once more. (With all tourists having been consigned to the other place, of course.)

The harbour had changed as greatly as had Port Llueso (the campaign to rename every place on the island with its Mallorquin form was being encouraged, to the confusion of everyone). When it had merely served the fishermen, it had consisted of two stone breakwaters, now it was a network of jetties at which were moored a bewildering variety of yachts and motor boats. Only a few years before, the water had been crystal clear, now it was virtually opaque and not even a starving Andaluz gitano would willingly eat any fish that came out of it.

Alvarez walked along the main western arm, past a restaurant whose prices were such that even if someone else had been paying the bill he would not have enjoyed the meal, to reach a boatyard. Two men were cleaning the keel of a yacht with very high-pressure water hoses. He asked where Delgado was. Not bothering to turn off his hose, shouting to overcome the noise, one man said the other was in the office.

Delgado was rich because he had the ability to impress a client with the belief that he put excellence before profit. That was why he dressed poorly, went to work in a rusting Panda and left the Mercedes at home, and frequently spoke of impending bankruptcy. Indeed, one yacht owner who boasted about the size of the debts he'd left in ports from

Bridgetown to Suva, was so moved by the sad story that he'd paid his account on the day it was presented.

When Alvarez walked into the small, cramped office, equipped with ancient battered equipment, Delgado was on the phone. After a moment, he replaced the receiver, leaned across the desk to shake hands. 'It's a difficult world,' he observed mournfully.

'Is the government increasing the wealth tax?'

'Probably, since they've increased every other one until a man can't afford to live, and can't afford to die.' He indicated the stained chair in front of the desk. 'What brings you here?'

'I'm looking for an Englishman.'

'Sadly, there's no lack of them.'

'Do you employ any?'

'Now that the rules have changed and it's no longer necessary to fake the work permits, I've three. So many boat owners don't speak Spanish that it's useful to have someone who can communicate. None of 'em does a proper day's work, of course.'

'That's fair enough, since you don't pay 'em a proper wage.'

'Always the humorist . . . What's the name of the Englishman you're looking for?'

'I don't know. Which is why I want you to call each one in turn in here so I can have a word with him.'

'Who pays for the lost time?'

'Charge it up to entertainment.'

Delgado stood, left. He returned a couple of minutes later. 'Bradley is out in the bay with a client, trying to find out why one of the engines is badly down on power, Hewitt and Burns are here. I've told 'em to come along one at a time, Hewitt first.'

Almost as Delgado finished speaking, a man in a heavily dirt-and-sweat stained boiler suit entered.

'You want something?' Hewitt asked, in inaccurate but recognizable Spanish, as he faced Delgado.

87

Alvarez said in English: 'In fact, señor, it is I who wish to speak to you.'

He turned. 'Yeah?' His thick features held sullen lines.

'I have a message for you from Señora Rachael.'

'Who? Don't know any bird of that name. And I never mess with marrieds. Not worth the aggro.'

'Then I'm sorry, there seems to have been a mistake.'

'Think nothing of it, squire. And if this Rachael has a younger sister who's not married, tell her I'm free between eight and nine tonight.' He swaggered out, a plebeian Don Juan.

'What was he saying?' Delgado asked. 'I couldn't understand much of it.'

'He could spare an hour this evening in which to pleasure a young lady.'

'Are you in the poncing business?'

'Would I be poor if I were?'

'Perhaps, since in this day and age few are willing to pay for what is freely available.' Delgado's tone became reflective. 'We have seen life change, you and me. When we were young, if we looked at a woman twice we became her novio and her mother was always there to make certain life was not full of pleasure. So it had to be the caseta with green shutters on the edge of the village when we could get a few pesetas together. But now the beaches are filled with women who flaunt what before was secret, their mothers are nowhere to be seen, and a man has no need to visit the caseta with green shutters. The young of today are luckier than rats in an almond tree.'

'Remember what the local priest used to tell us? Happiness lies through denial.'

'Can you ever remember his kind finding out if that were true?'

The door opened and a second man entered. Tall, broad shouldered, Marlboro-country handsome, he carried the air of a man who would respect authority only for as long as he agreed with it. He came to a stop by the side of Alvarez, faced Delgado.

'Señor Burns?' Alvarez said.

He half turned.

'I have a message for you from Señora Rachael.'

He showed his surprise. 'What is it?'

'Señor Cooper has disappeared.'

Despite his chunky features, he had an expressive face. It was not difficult to judge the point at which his puzzlement turned into suspicion. 'Who the hell are you?'

'Inspector Alvarez, Cuerpo General de Policia.'

'When did she give you the message?'

'Perhaps I should confess that the señora gave me no message. My little stratagem was to discover if you know her.'

'Your little stratagem is crap! What concern of yours is it if I do know her?'

'Perhaps you have not yet learned that the señor's car has been found and the circumstances suggest that he has committed suicide? It has become my task to try to find out why he should have had cause to take his own life.'

'Why should I be able to tell you anything about that?'

'You are a friend of the señora.'

'A casual friend.'

'What does that mean?'

'If we happen to meet, we have a coffee and a drink at one of the cafés. That's all.'

'You do not visit her at her house?'

'I went there once because her husband was thinking of buying a boat and needed advice.'

'That's the only time you've been there?'

'Isn't that what I've just said?'

'Then it was not you who was swimming there when the señor was away and the staff were not present and only the señora was there?'

He tried, but failed, to hide his consternation.

'I have been told that both the señora and you were without costumes.'

'Whoever it was told you that is a bloody liar.'

'Why should anyone lie about such things?'

'How the hell should I know? Maybe that's how they get their kicks. And even if we'd been updating the Kamasutra, what business is it of yours?'

'As I said earlier, my job is to try to discover why the señor might have committed suicide. If he had discovered that his wife and you were cuckolding him, that would be good cause.'

'I wasn't.'

'You are quite certain he did not discover the truth?'

'It's not the truth. It's something thought up by a god-damn pervert. Why can't you understand what I'm telling you?'

'I understand, but I have to consider whether I can believe it, because if the señor did not commit suicide, then . . .'

'You've just said he did.'

'I said that the circumstances suggest that he did. But circumstances can be carefully arranged.'

'What are you trying to suggest now?'

'That until I can be certain of the facts, I cannot uncover the truth. And that when a person lies, I have to wonder what can be his motive for doing so . . . Señor, let me ask you once more – did you visit Ca'n Oliver one Sunday when the señora was on her own and did she and you swim in the nude?'

'No.'

Was he lying merely to protect Rachael? 'Thank you for your help.'

Burns seemed to be about to speak, but then he turned and left the office.

'You talked too fast for me to understand anything,' Delgado complained. 'What was it all about?'

'Just a routine matter,' Alvarez replied.

'Since when would a man like him become so concerned over something that is routine? You were on about Señora Rachael, who is the wife of the man who has disappeared. What's Neil been up to – humping her when he gets the chance?'

'You've got a one-track mind.'

'Show me the man who hasn't.'

'What's Burns's address?'

'Why didn't you ask him for that?'

'I forgot.'

'Like hell! You just didn't want to let on that you were interested. You're a cunning bastard.'

Coming from Delgado, that was a compliment.

Alvarez drove down the harbour arm and then along the front road until he reached 157a. Here, half a kilometre from the centre of the tourist area, some of the older property remained and both 157 and 158 were two floors high, had outside staircases up to the top floors, and were in need of repairs to the exterior fabric. Outside 158, an old woman, dressed all in black, sat within the shade of the narrow, overhead patio. He crossed the wide pavement and came to a stop by the chair. 'Good morning.'

She stared at him with rheumy eyes, chewing on nothing with toothless gums. He greeted her a second time; she continued to stare silently at him and make no reply. Old age, the one disease that was only escaped through premature death, he thought, with an inward shudder.

A younger woman hurried out through the ground-floor doorway. 'She's deaf and away in the hills much of the time. What do you want?' She spoke with the nervous impatience of someone who was faced each day with a greater burden than she thought she could meet.

He introduced himself.

'What's wrong?' She looked nervously at her mother, who was alternately mumbling and grimacing.

'I just need to ask a couple of questions about someone else.'

She hesitated, finally said: 'You'd best come inside.'

He followed her into the front room, which had the minimum of furniture, but was spotlessly clean. 'You'll take a coñac?'

There would be little money in this house to spend on

drink and it might have seemed kinder to have refused the offer, but had he done so it would have been an indication that he was aware of her relative poverty and that would have mortified her. 'A very small one. I have an ulcer and have to be careful.'

'My husband also had ulcers and before he died, God rest his soul, he couldn't take any alcohol.'

'Then I must count myself fortunate.'

She went through to the back room, returned with a glass in which was a brandy as small, even, as those that were served in English bars. He wished her health, sipped the drink, encouraged her to tell him about the hardships of life, hoping that she would gain some slight, if illusory relief from them by doing so. It was not until many minutes later that he said: 'Does an Englishman live next door?'

She nodded. 'He rents the flat for thirty thousand a month. How can a man be so stupid as to pay that sort of money?'

How would she describe the foreigners who, at the height of the season, paid perhaps even as much as a million to rent the large villas with swimming pools and staff? 'Do you see much of him?'

'He has a chat now and then. Ma likes him, when she's in a state to like anyone, that is. Works in the boatyard. I told him, watch out for that one, Gregorio's a real fox! When I was young, he was the same as the rest of us, but now look at him. Lives in a palace and married to a forastero from the Peninsula. Like a stranger.'

The inrush of tourist money had bred such inequality, where before there had been the equality of poverty, that lifelong friendships had been sundered. 'Is the Englishman married?'

'Does any man marry when he can get what he wants and stay single?'

'He has girlfriends?'

'Call 'em that if you like. When I was young, we had a different name.'

'You see them often?'

'Me? I'm too busy to bother about such things, what with a job, the house, and Ma to look after. She sits out every day it's fine and if it's one of her good days she notices who goes up to his flat.'

'Has she seen anyone in the last few days?'

'Probably, but I wouldn't know for sure. Don't always listen too hard to what she's saying.'

'Would she be able to describe the most recent visitors?'

'Not today. Couldn't tell you who she is herself.'

'And you've not seen anyone?'

'Only the married one yesterday, when I rushed home for a bit.' She spoke with the scorn of a virtuous woman.

'How do you know she's married?'

'Got eyes in my head, haven't I? She's so brazen, she doesn't even take the ring off her finger.'

'Can you describe her?'

She did so.

He was disconcerted by the fact that she thought Rachael looked like a tart.

CHAPTER 13

Twenty-five years before, Cala Xima had been no more than a beach; now that it was a summer resort which lacked any roots in the past, its only character was the one provided by the tourists – the mindless pursuit of pleasure. Probably there was not, throughout the season, one tourist who knew, let alone was interested in, the fact that three kilometres inland there was a five thousand-year-old talayot that intrigued and puzzled archaeologists because of its unique form.

Alvarez parked his car and walked along the pavement. He passed a shop selling T-shirts with obscene messages in English, French, or German; a group of teenagers who forced him into the road; a woman, so obese that even a kaftan might not have been sufficient to preserve the susceptibilities of others, who wore a bikini-top and shorts; a man who had drunk himself into near insensibility. This was the price that had had to be paid for the huge material benefits which tourism had brought to the island; it was a price that his generation, but perhaps not the next, would rather had not been paid.

Garaje Xima stood on a corner site, one road back from the front. In one corner of the large open area, in which the hire cars were stored, was a small glassed-in office. A man in his early twenties, sleekly handsome and with the eager, predatory gaze of a committed one-night stander, was working at a computer. As Alvarez entered from the road, he studied Alvarez's appearance, looked back at the screen.

'I'd like some information.'

'Prices are in the folder. No cars available for the next five days.'

'I'm not after hiring a car.'

'Then why bother me?'

'Cuerpo General de Policia.'

He used his legs to swivel the chair round and stood to face Alvarez across the counter, watchful but not fearful, as he would probably have been in earlier times.

'I want to know if this car was hired from you and if so, the name and address of the hirer.'

'Has some stupid bastard crashed or tried to sell it?'

Alvarez passed across a slip of paper. 'That's the number.'

The man sat, tapped out instructions on the keyboard, read the screen. 'Ernest White. Hired the car on the thirteenth for eight days. Came in yesterday and extended the hiring for another week.'

'What nationality is he?'

'He's on an American driving licence and his passport's American.'

'His address?'

'We delivered the car to the Hotel Pedro.'

'Whereabouts is that?'

'Down to the front road, turn right, and it's just over half a kilometre along; you can't miss it. In some sort of trouble, is he?'

'Aren't we all?'

Alvarez returned to his car and drove past the usual depressing mixture of tourist shops, cafés and restaurants to the hotel. Set back from the road and fronted by neatly trimmed palms, the large building had considerable style, suggesting the architect had not been Mallorquin. Ignoring a notice directing all cars to the rear, he parked in the turning circle, climbed the marble steps, and entered the spacious foyer that was luxuriously furnished and had in the centre a fountain whose splashing water recalled the influence of the Moors. A hotel, of which there were gradually becoming more as the island tried to improve its image, which catered for holidaymakers who were prepared to pay more in order to be separated from those who would only pay less.

Despite the air-conditioning, the desk clerk, who wore a uniform of tie and dark-blue suit, had beads of sweat on his face. He listened to Alvarez, then spoke over the internal phone.

Alvarez was shown into a small office, where he was introduced to the assistant manager, a Dutchman who spoke five languages fluently and a couple more reasonably well and who had a manner which suggested that after several years in the hotel trade, he had heard and seen it all. 'There is some sort of problem?'

'This is just a routine inquiry,' Alvarez replied.

'The last "routine inquiry" with which I was concerned ended in a client falling out of a third-floor window as he tried to escape arrest for rape.'

'You can rest assured that in this case there has been no rape.'

'A reassurance that does, however, leave any number of other possibilities.'

When he judged that his unasked question was not going to be answered, he said: 'How exactly can I help you, Inspector?'

'I need to speak to Señor Ernest White, an American, who is probably staying here.'

The man tapped out instructions on the keyboard of the desk-top computer, read the information that came up on the VDU. 'We do have a guest by that name.'

'Can you check if he's in his room?'

He used the internal telephone to call room 432. 'No reply,' he said, as he replaced the receiver. 'Would you like me to have him paged?'

'Yes, please. And would it be possible to have a word with him in here?'

The assistant manager left. Alvarez wondered whether he'd have enjoyed working in the hotel business? Most hotels closed at the end of September and did not reopen until Easter, so that winter was one long holiday, subsidized by unemployment pay; there were tips; there were commissions to be discreetly earned; and even allowing for exaggerated hopes, it seemed there were many young romantics eager for passionate holiday romances . . . But during the season, it was all work; tips were earned by being deferential towards people to whom it would be a pleasure to be rude; all the worthwhile commissions were cornered by the concierge; and a man who was mature preferred quality to quantity in sex, as in most other things.

The door opened and the assistant manager briefly looked in. 'Señor White, Inspector.'

White entered, came forward with outstretched hand. 'The name's Ernest.'

All-American, Alvarez thought, as he shook hands and noticed the scar on the right cheek. But the blue eyes were not smiling, even if the mouth was, and they held a suggestion of watchful calculation. With nothing but these two facts and instinct to back his judgement, he identified White as either a criminal or someone with close connections with the criminal world.

'The hotel guy said you want to speak to me?'

'That's right. Thank you for coming, señor. Please sit.'

They both sat. 'Do you know Señor Cooper, who lives at Ca'n Oliver, in La Huerta de Llueso?'

'I guess so.'

'And you visited his house last Sunday, when you saw him, and last Tuesday, when you did not?'

'That's the way it went.'

'On Tuesday, Rosa, the maid, told you that he had disappeared?'

'Which sure surprised me.'

'I'm hoping you'll be able to help me discover the reason for his disappearance.'

'I doubt that, but anything I can do.'

'Have you seen him since you left Ca'n Oliver on Sunday?'

'Not so much as his shadow.'

'Have you any idea what may have happened to him?'

97

'I guess not.'

'You are a friend of long standing?'

'Never met the guy before Sunday.'

'Then what brought about the meeting?'

'I've a friend who knows him and when this friend heard I'd be on the island, he said to look up Oliver. So I arranged to visit him.'

'And how did the meeting go?'

'Like pork crackling at a Bar Mitzvah.'

'Why is that?'

'I'd kind of forgotten that the English don't take to sudden friendships and so what I met was polite reserve.'

'You're saying you had an argument?'

'Hell, no! If a guy doesn't want to pour me a second Scotch on the rocks, I'm not going to argue about it.'

'If you didn't have an argument, why did your visit so distress the señor?'

'I don't recollect saying it did.'

'Rosa told me that he appeared to be very upset by it.'

'I'd say she was mistaking distress for limey social disapproval. I wasn't wearing a coronet.' White was not trying to conceal his amused contempt for an islander who cut so different a picture from the conventional one of the hard, fast-talking detective.

'You hired a car from Garaje Xima on the thirteenth.'

'Sure.'

'For eight days?'

'That's important?'

'I don't know.'

'That makes two of us!'

'Presumably, you originally thought you would only be staying for eight days?'

'I guess that's a fair enough assumption.'

'Yesterday, you decided you would be staying for longer?'

'Right again.'

'What changed your mind?'

'There's more to see on the island than I thought.'

'Did you fly direct from America to here?'

'Via Madrid.'

'For what dates did you book your air ticket?'

For the first time, White hesitated. Then, as if to cover up this brief moment of doubt, he spoke with added casual humour. 'For eight days. But it's open-ended, so even if it bothered the clerk who didn't seem to know what it was, there's no problem.'

'And no problem either about staying longer away from America than you'd intended?'

'That's the way it is.'

'Then you have a very convenient job.'

'If I knew what that meant, I could answer.'

'I must apologize for my English, señor.'

'From where I sit, there's no call for apologies.'

'What I was trying to say is, you obviously have a job which allows you unexpectedly to take a longer holiday than intended.'

'I work for myself, so the boss is flexible.' He smiled.

'What kind of work do you do, señor?'

'Sales.'

'In which area?'

'The garment trade.'

'Thank you. I think that is all I need to ask.'

White stood, his movements smooth and quick. 'Sorry I can't be more helpful.'

'And I am sorry to have had to disturb you.'

He began to cross to the door.

'I have a memory like a mosquito net!' Alvarez suddenly said. 'There is something more I have to ask.'

White turned. 'Name it.'

'Did you visit Llueso before last Sunday?'

'I drove through it.'

'For any particular reason?'

'A guy in the hotel said not to miss Parelona. Seemed a good idea to take a look at the place on the way. '

'Did you stop in the village?'

99

'Might have had a coffee at a café . . . Your "something more" stretches a long way.'

'Forgive me, but sometimes one question calls for many answers. Since you may have stopped for a coffee, perhaps you decided also to find out where Señor Cooper lived so that you could study his house through binoculars?'

'Are you on the level? Why should I do that?'

'That is my next question.'

'Then the answer comes short. I didn't.'

'A man was seen studying the señor's house through binoculars.'

'Great. Only it wasn't yours truly.'

'The description of this man fits you, even down to the scar on your right cheek.'

'I guess you've been talking to someone with a great imagination.'

'What was your reason for visiting Señor Cooper?'

'I've told you.'

'What did you say to frighten him?'

White shrugged his shoulders in a gesture of tired impatience.

'Since you extended the hire of the car for another eight days as from yesterday, I imagine you have done the same with your airplane ticket. So if I ask you not to leave the island for at least the next six days, this will not cause any inconvenience?'

White, balancing himself on the balls of his feet as a man did when he was preparing to attack or defend himself, said, 'Are you trying to arrest me?' There was no trace of condescending humour in his manner now; only cold, hard calculation.

'Just because a few more questions may need answering? Of course not, señor. All I'm asking you to do is to be ready to help with the investigation, if you can.'

'If you're not arresting me, I'll leave when I want,' he said flatly.

'I'm afraid not.'

'After I've found a mouthpiece, you'll discover just how goddamn wrong you are.'

'I fear that lawyers here do not always have the same sense of professional urgency that they have in the television from your country, and should you consult one, it would probably take him many days to bring his mind to bear on your problem. But in order to make certain you are not tempted to prove me wrong and leave before the six days are up, I shall ask you for your passport.'

Just for a moment, White looked as if he would react with physical violence.

Because he had been born and brought up on the Peninsula, and had taken his law degree at Barcelona University, Gallardo had no complex and interlocking web of relatives on the island, all of whose interests had to be considered if there were any danger of their conflicting with those of his clients; he was thus able to offer unbiased legal advice to foreigners, an unusual fact which ensured that he received much of their work.

He shook hands with Alvarez, indicated the seat in front of the desk, sat, and listened with his egg-shaped head tilted to one side. He nodded. 'I handled the purchase of Señor Cooper's home and advised him that it was essential he made a Spanish will since he now owned property in Spain.'

'Will you give me the details of that will?'

'You think . . . ?'

'At the moment, I think nothing.'

'It's a wise man who can learn to do that.' He picked up the receiver, pressed down a switch on the base, spoke to his secretary.

In under a minute, a young woman, neatly dressed, entered and put a file down on the desk, left. Gallardo searched through the papers in the file, extracted one and read it. 'Short and to the point. Everything is left to the wife.'

'No other bequests?'

101

'None.'

'Have you any idea what size the estate is likely to be?'

He shook his head. 'I suppose the house is worth around a hundred million pesetas, but beyond that, who's to know? The señor will have kept his liquid assets in another country so that the Spanish tax bandits can't touch them. They must amount to two or three times as much, at the very least.'

Three, four, five hundred million. Murders had been committed for a fraction of that sum.

CHAPTER 14

As Alvarez entered the post, the duty cabo behind the desk looked up from his girlie magazine. 'You've become very popular.'

Alvarez came to a stop, mopped his face with a handkerchief.

'She's been in twice, asking for you. I told her not to waste her talents on a brass oldie. She didn't seem to understand.'

'Who are you talking about?'

'This foreign piece. She told me her name, but I've forgotten it. If she'd not given me thoughts, maybe I'd have remembered it.'

'Señora Cooper?'

'That sounds about right.'

'Did she leave a message?'

'Yes. But not in words.'

Alvarez carried on, climbed the stairs, and went along to his office. He settled in the chair behind the desk. No wonder the world was hellbent for trouble when the younger generation could think of nothing except sex. Not for them the demands and therefore the satisfactions of duty done; not for them . . . As he began to drift off to sleep, an image of Rachael as she climbed out of the pool slid into his mind . . .

The phone jerked him fully awake. Traffic reported that the most careful search had failed to uncover anything more of significance on or in the BMW.

Sometimes, nothing could be as significant as something; in this instance it was not. Had Cooper committed suicide, it was very unlikely there would be any traces beyond those already found. If he had been murdered, the murderer, wishing to set the scene for suicide, would surely have killed him and then either wrapped his corpse in a body-bag so that no traces could be left in the BMW, or, if he had had an accomplice, have transported it in another vehicle . . .

The internal phone rang. 'She's back,' said the duty cabo.

'Who are you talking about?'

'It's blokes like you give stupidity a bad name . . . Señora Cooper is here and wishes to speak to the inspector.'

Alvarez left the room and went down the stairs. The duty cabo was exerting all the charm of which he considered he had an abundance, but with little impact because in his eagerness he was speaking too quickly and using the flowery language of the traditional lover so that Rachael failed to understand much of what he said.

She swung round to face Alvarez. 'What d'you think you've been doing? When my husband comes back, he'll complain to the British ambassador in Madrid . . .'

'Señora, would it not be best if we go upstairs to my office where we can speak more privately?'

She hesitated.

'If you will go up those stairs.' He gestured with his hand.

She walked forward.

When satisfied she was out of earshot, the cabo muttered: 'What a waste on an old man like you.'

In the office, Alvarez moved the spare chair so that she could sit directly in front of the desk, then settled behind it. 'Please tell me, señora, what bothers you?'

'You know damn well! When you spoke to Neil this morning, you made the most disgusting accusation. Oliver's missing, I'm sick with worry, and all you can do is suggest I'm having an affair. Oh, God, why do I have to suffer such a nightmare? As if I could even think of betraying Oliver. How can you be so cruel?' She leaned forward and buried her face in her hands, shoulders shaking.

'Señora, please understand that I have to learn the truth. I make no moral judgements.'

'When you asked Neil all those filthy questions, you were making one,' she retorted, her voice muffled.

'I asked them in order to learn the facts because when those are known I will be better able to judge what has happened to your husband.'

She lifted her head, straightened her shoulders, brushed both cheeks with crooked right forefinger, although no tears had been obvious. 'I have been faithful to Oliver from the day I met him. Neil is a friend, nothing more. Or can't you conceive that a married woman can be friendly with another man and yet wouldn't have an affair with him in a million years?'

'I fear that it is in the nature of my job always to have to envisage the worst rather than the best. But in order that I may have the pleasure of acknowledging the best, will you answer a few questions?'

She hesitated as she considered his somewhat convoluted question, then said: 'I'll tell you everything I can.'

'Has Señor Burns ever visited Ca'n Oliver?'

'When Oliver was thinking of buying a boat and wanted to know what kind would best suit him, Neil came to the house to discuss the question and advise him.'

'Has Señor Burns been there at any other time?'

'He has not and he told you that. And as for someone saying we were swimming together naked, that's a beastly, filthy lie.'

'Why should anyone tell such a lie?'

'People can be so horrible. I suppose it was a man?'

'Yes.'

'Then obviously he's a pervert who gets his pleasure out of making disgusting allegations.'

'You have never swum naked in the pool at Ca'n Oliver with Señor Burns?'

'I've never swum in the pool with him, naked or in an Edwardian costume down below my knees.'

'Have you been having an affair with him?'

105

'Haven't I been telling you again and again that I haven't? What is it? You don't want to believe me because you also get your pleasure in funny ways?'

'Señora, I would very much like to believe you. Only before I can do that, I have to understand why you so frequently visit Señor Burns's flat in the port.'

The question shocked her and left her mentally scrambled. It was many seconds before she said: 'That . . . that's another horrible lie.' She recovered her poise and spoke far more certainly. 'Who suggested that? The same man?'

'Two ladies who have often seen you arrive or leave.'

'If you mean the woman who lives next door to Neil, he's told me that the old one is so gaga she sees flying saucers every day.'

'I understand that there are times when her mind is coherent. In any case, her daughter has confirmed that you have made many visits to the señor's flat.'

Her expression betrayed the panicky confusion in her mind, then she once more buried her face in her hands and this time cried genuine tears.

He stared past her and through the window. Tears of remorse, or tears of angry, bitter resentment at being found out? Love offered a path to heaven and a slide down to hell.

He reached down to his right and pulled open the bottom drawer, brought out a bottle of 103 and two glasses. Both glasses were dirty, so he cleaned one with his handkerchief, holding it below the level of the desk as he did so. He poured out two drinks, carried one glass around the desk to her. 'Señora, drink this.'

After a moment, she took the glass. She stared at it for a while before she drank. 'You've got to understand,' she said urgently.

'I will certainly try to.'

Her voice dulled. 'You've already made up your mind what kind of a person I am.'

'Señora, we have a saying, Before you judge someone,

106

be sure you are ready to be judged. I am not ready.'

She stared ahead of her with unfocused gaze. 'Life here was so different from life in England; there it's perpetual winter, here it's perpetual summer. I felt ten times more alive; I wanted to capture moonbeams and ride on stars . . . Do I sound very stupid?'

'Far from it.'

'Parties were supercharged and men flirted outrageously, which was flattering and exciting, but initially I was scared Oliver would take that seriously. But he never said anything, anything at all, and it was as if he didn't bother to notice. That hurt. I set out to try to provoke him and make him admit he was jealous, but he still didn't respond. I decided that all he felt was pride that so many men admired me; he was seeing me as one of his possessions and was gratified that people envied him. It made me feel . . .

'I'd only once seen Neil before the Phelps gave a party and that was when he came to the house to talk to Oliver about boats. None of our English friends ever invited him because he'd no money and had to earn a living. But the Phelps are American and see things in a different light; they look down on people who don't work. They invited him because he'd done some repairs to their boat and they thought him a real craftsman and they liked him.

'He was so obviously being cold-shouldered by all those Brits who even felt demeaned by his being there and I made a point of going over and talking to him . . . Can you remember what it's like when you're with someone and suddenly there's electricity?'

Why, he wondered gloomily, did she use the past tense?

'Neil phoned me the next day and asked me out for a drink. I refused. He rang the next day and then the day after that and he told me that I had to agree in order to prove the truth that it was third time lucky. That . . . that's how it happened.'

'Does your husband suspect?'

'No.'

'How can you be so certain?'

107

'I've always told him I'm seeing a friend and she's backed me up. He's such a snob he wouldn't allow himself even to begin to doubt her word.'

'So clearly it's been very much in your interests that the truth has been concealed from him.'

Her voice rose. 'You're not . . . not thinking I could ever do something terrible to prevent him learning?'

'Sadly, that is one possibility I have to consider.'

'But I love him.'

His expression was more revealing than he'd hoped.

'You think I'm the complete bitch!'

'Señora . . .'

'You just don't want to understand.'

'Understand what?'

'That a person can suffer brief madness and then spend the rest of her life regretting it.'

'This was only a brief affair?'

She stared at him with a look of dismay. 'You believe I could go on and on deceiving Oliver? Can you not see what sort of a person I really am?'

'You've visited Señor Burns's flat very recently.'

'And absolutely nothing happened. I just needed to speak to him about something . . . All right, I made a fool of myself; all right, I betrayed Oliver and summer madness is no real excuse. But I came to my senses and ended everything before Oliver so much as suspected.' She stared at him, her deep blue eyes fixed on his. 'I couldn't let Oliver be hurt. That was more important than anything else.' She waited, then said in a pleading voice: 'Please, will you be kind?'

'In what way?'

'When Oliver returns, don't tell him what I've just told you. It could only hurt him most terribly to know and knowing can't change anything.'

'Unless circumstances force me to tell him, I won't.'

'You've made me feel as if I've been to confession and you've absolved me and now I can start life again with a clean slate.'

It was unfortunate that she should cast him in the role of a priest; something less, as well as something more, than a man.

'Please find him quickly.'

'To help me do that, tell me one or two things. Does your husband smoke?'

'Yes, he does. I keep telling him he must give it up for the sake of his health, but he won't.'

'Does he smoke one particular brand?'

'When he can get them, it's always Lucky Strike.'

'And which whisky does he normally drink?'

'He never drinks it because he doesn't like it.'

Alvarez fidgeted with a pencil. 'I know it must sound stupid to ask this, but could you perhaps be mistaken?'

'No, I couldn't.'

'Then there is a problem.'

'What problem?'

'As to why there was an empty bottle of whisky in his car. Of course, he may previously have had a passenger who for some reason left it there.'

'Oliver's far too fussily tidy to overlook an empty bottle.'

'Then I must look for the explanation somewhere else.'

'I don't really understand.' She stood. 'It helps to know you're doing everything possible.'

'I am glad of that, señora.'

He escorted her downstairs and out to the road. When he returned, the duty cabo said: 'So was it as good as it looks?'

He walked on.

It was a long-recognized fact that the more unwelcome an event, the more certainly it would occur at the most inconvenient moment. Alvarez was about to return home – perhaps a little early, but it had been a wearing day – when the phone rang and the plum-voiced secretary said that the superior chief wished to speak to him.

'What the devil's going on?' were the superior chief's opening words.

'In what respect, señor?'

'In every respect.'

'I'm afraid I don't quite follow.'

'Not an uncommon occurrence. Some time ago, you reported that an Englishman had disappeared, yet I have received no report on the matter. Why not?'

'I thought it best to complete my preliminary investigation, señor, before submitting one. And since the car was found only yesterday . . .'

'What car?'

'The señor's BMW.'

'Would it cause you any concern to learn that until now I had not the slightest idea it had been found?'

'I presumed Traffic would have told you.'

'Assume far less, ascertain far more. I suggest you now detail all the facts, leaving aside all assumptions.'

Alvarez did so.

'You remain convinced the Englishman is dead?'

He did not reply immediately.

'Well?'

'Señor, since there is no direct proof he is dead, I can only note the surrounding circumstances and on them make an assumption. Yet you have just made it clear that I am to assume nothing . . .'

'There are times, Alvarez, when I find it difficult to decide whether you suffer from a lack of intelligence or perversely set out to irritate. Is it not obvious that I was referring to assumptions which are totally unjustified?'

'Yet how does one judge if they are justified or unjustified if one does not know all the facts; and if one does know them all, then surely there can be no need to assume?'

Salas said wearily: 'Just tell me whether you think he is dead or alive.'

'I think he must be dead. Would a man willingly leave in ignorance the wife he loved? Would a rich man choose to disappear within a few hours of flying to England in order to set out on a luxury cruise which has no doubt cost many millions of pesetas?'

'Assume he is dead.'

'Then the question becomes, did he commit suicide or was he murdered? The circumstances appear to point to suicide. The car was very close to a cliff and the newspaper article recorded a suicide by jumping over a cliff; an empty bottle of whisky and evidence of the taking in quantity some form of medicinal drug, probably a sedative, suggests he dulled his senses in order to bring himself to take the final step. Yet I have been unable to uncover any reason for his committing suicide, he suffers from altophobia and so would he choose a form of death that must entail extra horror? He left no suicide note, which is unusual, and he never drinks whisky. Faced with these inconsistencies, I believe he was murdered by someone who set out to make his death look like suicide.'

'Someone who did not know him very well.'

'Or someone who knows him well, but wishes to make out that the murderer did not.'

'If he was murdered, there has to be a motive.'

'Indeed.'

'In the course of your prolonged investigation, have you identified anyone with one?'

'There are four, maybe five, such persons. You will remember my telling you that his wife had been observed swimming in the nude with a man other than her husband. I have identified the man and confirmed that they were having an affair. She claims that it was a very brief affair and is long since over. However, Señor Cooper was wealthy and she is the sole beneficiary under the will. Financially, it is in her interests for the señor to have died and, if one projects, equally in the interests of Señor Burns, her paramour. Secondly, there is an American, Señor White, whose visit on the Sunday seems to have frightened Señor Cooper to the extent that he left the house, although lunch was soon to be served. Señor White maintains the only reason for his visit was that friends suggested he called. I'm of the opinion that Señor White has criminal connections, although at the moment I have no proof of that. I have impounded his passport and would request that the American authorities be asked if he is known to them. Then there is Serra, a local farmer, who is very bitter because Señor Cooper has stopped his receiving the water which legally is Señor Cooper's.'

'This is the first time I've heard that the failure to receive something to which one has no entitlement can be a valid motive for murder.'

'It is more complicated than it seems.'

'That can be taken as read since you are handling the investigation.'

'Water has always been a source of trouble and in the past many men have been killed in arguments over the rights. I can remember my grandfather telling me . . .'

'I do not think we need to occupy ourselves with family reminiscences. Have you questioned this farmer?'

'Not yet.'

'Why not, if you somehow manage to regard him as a possible suspect?'

'I haven't had the time . . .'

'The mark of an efficient officer is that he makes time. Even when it is only to follow up an idea that would seem absurd to anyone unacquainted with this island and its inhabitants. And the fifth possibility?'

'A long-time friend of Señor Cooper's, Señor Field.'

'What is his motive?'

'He has none as far as I have been able to ascertain. In fact, quite the opposite; it was in his interests for the señor to continue to live.'

'Then why name him?'

'He would know better than most how to make it appear that he knew nothing.'

'On that score, you can add a sixth suspect. Yourself.' Salas cut the connection.

CHAPTER 15

Even Jaime admitted that there were times when Dolores relaxed and openly allowed her fierce love for the family to envelop them all and touch them with the same deep happiness that she enjoyed. It was then that her cooking reached such heights that the gods would have forsaken Olympus to dine at her table.

Alvarez lay on his bed, stared up at the ceiling, and decided that the dinner they had earlier eaten had lifted them to the pinnacle of human experience. Not even love could offer so clear a vision of paradise, since women sadly carried within themselves the seeds of the poison of possessiveness . . . At such a time, one should be generous. It wasn't always the woman's fault that love turned into a dagger. A man could be to blame. He drifted off to sleep, congratulating himself on his fair-mindedness . . .

He was awoken by the distant sounds of the telephone ringing. With the shutters closed, the light in the bedroom was dim, yet it was sufficient for him to read the non-luminous dial of his watch. 6.14. For anyone to ring this early in the morning there surely had to be an emergency. He mentally checked. Isabel and Juan had returned home and gone safely to bed the previous night; it was inconceivable that either of them would have risen so early and gone into the street to be run over. Dolores wouldn't leave the house before she'd prepared everyone's breakfast or Jaime until he'd eaten his. No immediate family could be involved . . .

'Enrique.'

The call was for him? 'Who is it?' he shouted back.

'A woman.'

Dolores had only spoken the two words and her voice had been muffled by distance, but even so he knew exactly what she was thinking. Why, he wondered as he left the bed, was the virtuous woman so quick to presume vice?

She was climbing the stairs as he reached the head and he stood to one side. 'She has woken everyone up by ringing at such an absurd hour,' she said, as she stepped on to the landing.

'I'm very sorry, but . . .'

'Tell her, if she is capable of understanding, that there are people whose work is by day and who therefore need to sleep at night.'

'It must be some kind of emergency.'

'Perhaps. But I shall not be too surprised if it proves to be otherwise,' she said, words crackling icily. She studied him briefly. 'Could you not have put on a dressing-gown since you are wearing only pyjama trousers?'

'There's only the family . . .'

'Whom I have to do everything in my power to protect.' She swept on and along to her bedroom.

Sweet Mary, but it was as impossible to understand a woman's mind as foretell in which direction a flea would jump.

He went downstairs and through to the front room, picked up the receiver. 'Enrique Alvarez speaking.'

'Oh, God, someone's killed him. His head . . .' She began to make a sound that was half sob, half cry.

There was a pause, then another voice came on the line. 'You must come here.'

'Who's speaking?'

'Rosa.'

'What exactly has happened?'

'The señor's lying there, his head . . . It's terrible,' she said, her voice beginning to tremble.

Where had the body been hidden? An attic, a seldom-opened cupboard; who had visited the hiding place so early in the morning? 'Rosa, try to be very calm.'

114

'But . . . but it's so awful . . .'

'I am sure you can be brave. Tell me, is the body in the house or the garden?'

'The house.'

'Whereabouts?'

'In the señor's dressing-room. On . . . on the floor.'

His response was immediate. 'That's impossible.'

'I tell you, the señor's on the floor. Haven't I seen him, lying there, his head . . . Oh, God, his head!'

It had never occurred to him to search the house because Cooper had been last seen leaving it and that fact had fixed in his mind the presumption that the other had died elsewhere. 'Hasn't anyone been in the dressing-room in the past four days?'

'I can't say when the señora was there . . .'

'Of course you can't. But what about you or Clara?'

'Yesterday.'

'How d'you mean?'

'We clean every day except Sunday. I dusted and hoovered in there in the morning. And now he's lying there and his head . . . his head . . .'

Alvarez said what he could to calm her. As he replaced the receiver, he wondered how he was going to calm Salas?

The very large bedroom was furnished with luxurious taste. The wide double bed was an antique Spanish half tester, the counterpane was made from the finest Mallorquin crochetwork; the large carpet was a Sanguzsko; two easy chairs were velvet covered, the heavy curtains had elaborate pelmets; the central ceiling light was a crystal chandelier, its graceful proportions preventing it looking pretentious; on the walls hung three paintings, so similar in style that they were clearly by the same artist – millennium-old, twisted olive trees were the favoured staple of island painters, but this artist possessed the skill to banish any sense of cliché.

On one side of the bedroom was a bathroom, fully tiled in marble and with deep-burgundy-coloured fittings, on the other was the dressing-room. Cooper lay in an untidy heap on an uncarpeted section of the floor, his left hand curled under his body, his right hand stretched out and almost touching the elaborately inlaid, highly polished dressing-table set in front of the window. Two full-length mirrors, one on each of the side walls, reflected the body, surrounding the onlooker with death.

Cooper wore a short-sleeved silk shirt and linen trousers. His skull had been savaged, but despite this fact, the wounds were not as visually horrific as they might have been. His expression was one more of surprise than horror. The floor around his head was stained with blood.

After three and a half days in the heat, one would have expected to see the first signs of staining on the visible flesh. There was none. The blood had not started to degenerate, either on the body or floor. Alvarez tried to move first one arm, then the other, but both had become locked by rigor. He straightened up. Cooper had not been murdered on the Sunday and his body hidden until now; he had died within the last twenty-four hours or less, depending on when Rosa had cleaned the room. Had he returned willingly – if so, why had he ever left? Had he been forced to return – if so, why and by whom? That he had bled on to the floor and that the pattern suggested no subsequent disturbance, suggested he had not been killed elsewhere and his body brought here. How could he have returned to the house without anyone's knowing that? Who did, and who did not, have an alibi? And finally, remembering the one question Salas must ask, could this be accident or suicide? No surface on any of the built-in cupboards or the dressing-table bore any imprint, suggesting he had fallen on to that. As for suicide? Nothing which could have inflicted the injury (and although he was no doctor, he was certain the wounds could not have been self-inflicted) lay about the floor.

He walked over to the window and stared out, mentally listing what had to be done. Telephone a doctor who'd make the preliminary examination and give a working time of death. Search the house for any signs of forced entry. Question all those known to have a motive for Cooper's death to find out if they had alibis. Exactly who stood to benefit from the death? What had been the true reason for the meeting between Cooper and White? Did White have criminal connections? . . .

Doctors who worked within the national health service were contractually obliged to give only a proportion of their working time to that service and were allowed to carry on a contiguously timed private practice. However, it was base calumny to suggest that there were those among the profession who demanded payment before committing their best efforts.

Dr Pons wore a suit even in the height of summer, since it marked the distinction between himself and the common man. He straightened up, dusted the knees of his trousers with his hands. 'You can turn him over.'

Alvarez, trying hard to think of the body as a thing, not a dead man, sweated heavily as he struggled to move it, a task made difficult because of the stiffened arm.

'You're badly out of condition,' Pons observed.

The task would have stressed him considerably less had the other deigned to give a hand.

'D'you smoke?'

'A little.'

'D'you drink?'

'Occasionally.'

'Give up both, take exercise, and you might just live for another ten years.'

'But would they be worth living?'

Pons had a poor sense of humour and saw the question as impudent. He waited in disapproving silence until the body had been turned and he could continue his examination. After a while, he said: 'Do you see that?'

Alvarez moved forward and looked at the watch on the left wrist which had been concealed previously. The glass

117

had been shattered and the sweep second hand was bent and motionless.

'You will appreciate the significance of this, of course. In all probability, it marks the time of death.'

'Nine twenty-three comes within the estimate of the time of death that you've gained from the usual indicators?'

'Yes.' The doctor stood, replaced the instruments in his case, peeled off the surgical gloves, dusted his trousers. 'They provide a time of between nine and midnight.'

'Can you give me the cause of death?'

'That is not obvious?'

'I have to have your given opinion for the records.'

'He was struck repeatedly, but the apparent injuries inflicted are less than I would have expected to have caused death, suggesting that the dead man has an unusually fragile skull. It is my opinion that the number and nature of the blows points to loss of self-control on the part of the assailant. That is all that can be said before the post-mortem.' He picked up his bag, left, walking with short, springy steps.

Alvarez locked the dressing-room and pocketed the key. He sat on one of the bedroom chairs. Still to organize were tests for prints, the taking of photographs, questioning the señora and the staff, questioning those known to have a motive . . .

Would Rosa offer him a coffee and a coñac before he set forth?

The photographer had taken photographs, the dressing-room had been dusted for prints and those raised had been lifted on sticky tape, the señora's doctor had said she could not be questioned before the late afternoon at the earliest. So now he had to make that telephone call.

He used the cordless telephone in the sitting-room. The plum-voiced secretary told him to wait. He waited, his mind wandering.

'Well?'

The barked question startled him and it was a moment before he could say: 'I have to report that Señor Cooper is dead.'

'You have forgotten that you first reported this fact several days ago?'

'Previously, señor, as I made clear, his death could only be surmised. Now, it is definite. The circumstances make it certain he was murdered.'

'There can be no doubt that he fell accidentally or deliberately jumped?'

'He did not fall over the cliff.'

'Then where did he die?'

'In his dressing-room.'

There was a silence. 'You had not, of course, thought to search there?'

'Señor, he was known to have left home . . .'

'I should blame myself. I should have explained as simply as possible what you should do, even to the extent of advising the necessity of so elementary a task as searching the house.'

'I would not have found him.'

'I'm sure that's correct. However, someone more alert would have done.'

'No one would have found him because he wasn't there.'

'Forgive me, Alvarez, but at this relatively early hour in the morning I am finding it rather difficult to understand you. Are you, in inimitable style, reporting the fact that the body had been moved to where it was found?'

'Señor Cooper died last night, possibly at nine twenty-three.'

There was a longer silence. 'You are now saying that for several days you have been investigating the murder of someone who was alive?'

'In a sense, señor. But it has not been time wasted.'

'That has to be a matter of opinion.'

'My previous work has enabled me to discover who has a motive for the señor's death.'

119

'I had forgotten. You claim to have identified a man willing to murder for a bucketful of water.'

'Señor, in the old days when a farmer could only rely on what he, himself, produced . . .'

'I am sure we can find more important things to discuss than the hydraulic history of a backward island. Has the body been medically examined?'

'Yes, señor.'

'Have photographs been taken?'

'Yes, señor.'

'Have all relevant surfaces been examined for finger-prints and other marks?'

'Yes, señor.'

'Has the Institute of Forensic Anatomy been notified that a full postmortem will be required?'

'Yes, señor.'

'*Mirabile dictu.*' He cut the connection.

As Alvarez replaced the receiver, he belatedly realized that he had forgotten to confirm with Salas that a request for information concerning White had been made to the American authorities. He judged it advisable not to ring back.

CHAPTER 16

Clara, being considerably older than Rosa, could remember a time when no sensible person spoke his mind except in the company of trusted friends – how else to be certain that the secret police were not listening? So it was only after Alvarez had chatted to her for some time that he was able to persuade her to speak relatively freely.

'He sounds like he was a difficult man,' he said, as he sat at the kitchen table.

'He could be, that's for sure. Never said how delicious the meals were.'

A good cook needed imagination, inspiration, forty-three spices, and praise without end. 'Wasn't he interested in food?'

'He was quick enough to say if he didn't like something.'

'The typical foreigner! . . . Did Rosa have any trouble with him?'

'Not if you mean, did he try to get a handful. She'd have told him what was what. In any case, if you ask me, the señor didn't think of us as ordinary sort of people. We're servants. Another thing. He'd the señora to keep him happy.'

'D'you reckon she did?'

'As busy as he could manage.'

'I've been told she has a friend and sometimes, when they're alone, they have a swim together?'

'So Jorge says, but he has an imagination that needs washing.'

'Only it's not imagination this time. D'you think the señor knew she was dancing to someone else's band?'

She accepted that there was small point in continuing

loyally to deny the affair. 'If he'd had his wits about him, he'd have guessed right enough from the way she made an extra fuss of him. But being the man he was, he just thought that that was because she adored him even more. Many's the time I've said to Rosa that England must be a strange country when someone as blind as him can become so rich.'

'In any country, when a woman puts her body as well as her mind to it, she can make a man believe the earth is square.'

'Until she starts carrying a bastard.'

'Life can be full of little surprises . . . So you don't think he ever suspected?'

'If he had, he'd have been shouting the house down. Men like him can't stand being made to look stupid.'

'Tell me, were you in this house last night?'

Her manner changed abruptly. She stared nervously everywhere but at him and began to fiddle with a small bowl that was on the table.

'There's no need to worry,' he assured her. 'I could never believe you had any part in the señor's death. What I'm asking is if you were here, you saw or heard anything unusual?'

'There was nothing.'

'Suppose you just remember everything you can about yesterday evening. It's as important to me to know everything seemed normal as that there was something strange. The kind of thing I want to hear is who was around, what you were doing, whether anyone telephoned.'

She spoke hesitantly to begin with, then gained confidence. The señora had left the house soon after breakfast without saying what she wanted for the day. Unless there was a party, only she or Rosa had to be on duty during the evening and so Rosa had left quite early to be with her novio. She'd spent the early evening worrying. Should she prepare dinner or shouldn't she? If she did and the señora didn't want a meal when she returned, it would be food wasted; if she didn't and the señora demanded a meal immediately, there would be a row. The señora expected everything to be exactly as she wanted . . .

Eventually, it had become clear that the señora would not be returning for dinner – it was always served at the same time, on the señor's orders. So she'd locked up, after switching on the alarm system, and had left and gone to the staff house. She'd watched television for a while and then decided to get some supper. After switching off the television, she'd heard a car. She'd thought it was the señora's, but when she'd crossed to the window and looked out, she'd seen it wasn't and the car was leaving, not arriving – she hadn't heard it before because of the television and, she had to admit, she wasn't as sharp of hearing as she'd once been . . .

'Have you any idea whose car it was?'

'Señor Field's,' she answered immediately.

'I gather he's a good friend of the señor?'

'A lot better friend to both of 'em than they are to him. Leastwise, the señora. She sometimes treats him like . . . Well, like one of us.'

'Have you any idea what the time was when he was here?'

'Not really.'

'Was he driving very quickly?'

She considered the question for some time. 'He never drives fast. If you ask me, that wouldn't be safe in his car.'

'Have you any idea when Señor Cooper returned here?'

'How could I have?' she asked, suddenly once more alarmed.

'I just thought you might have heard the car, that's all.'

She shook her head.

'When did you leave here last evening and go to the staff house?'

'Just after half past eight.'

'And apart from Señor Field's car, you neither saw nor heard anything or anybody?'

'That's right.' She stared into space. 'Who . . . who'd want to do so terrible a thing?'

'You can't think of anyone who might?'

Her expression became blank.

He wondered of whom she was thinking? Rachael and Burns; White; Serra? Did she realize the significance of her evidence concerning Field's visit? It was impossible to guess, let alone judge.

Farmhouses and casetas had normally been built on the boundaries of the properties in order to 'waste' as little land as possible. Since no building on a boundary was allowed to have a window that overlooked adjoining land, one side had to be blank. Ca Na Ia, reached by a dirt track, stood on the edge of a field. Originally a rock-built caseta offering the minimum accommodation and no comfort – one bedroom, one main room, one kitchen, and a long drop – it had been enlarged and modernized, but this had been done with such sympathetic care that that fact was not immediately apparent. It was surrounded on three sides by a narrow garden that consisted neither of the Mallorquin haphazard mixture of flowers and vegetables, nor the regimented flower beds of the suburban expatriates.

Field came round the corner of the building as Alvarez climbed out of his Ibiza, parked alongside the Seat 127. 'Good morning,' he said in Spanish.

Once again, Alvarez was impressed that here was a man who took the trouble to speak Castilian. 'I'm sorry about the death of your friend,' he said, as he shook hands.

'Thank you . . . Is the rumour that he was murdered true?'

'I fear so.'

'I was hoping . . .' Field stared at the nearest fig tree. 'Emotion can make one very illogical. Why should suicide seem less horrible than murder?'

'Because one can hope that suicide brings the relief that was being sought?'

'Perhaps . . . Let's get out of the sun.' He led the way around the side of the caseta. In the centre of the small lawn there was a palm tree and a chair had been set out in its shade.

'Do sit down. I'll get another chair from inside. And what can I offer you to drink?'

'May I have a coñac?'

'With soda or ginger ale?'

'With just ice, please.'

Field went inside. Alvarez settled in the chair. A sparrow landed on the sawn-off stub of one of last year's fronds and dabbed its beak, searching for food; another landed further down and was immediately chased away. There was probably more than enough food for them both, but in nature the strong usually denied the weak . . .

Field brought out a small table and folding chair and set them down, returned inside for a tray on which were two glasses and a plateful of olives. He passed a glass to Alvarez, sat. 'Help yourself to olives – I bought them in the market on Sunday and they've still got their stones in, so beware teeth.'

The pleasure of the iced brandy, tart olives, and the shade, were such that it needed a conscious effort on Alvarez's part to remember that this was not a social occasion. 'I fear I have to ask you some questions.'

'Of course. But first, may I put one? How did Oliver die?'

'All I can be certain of at the moment is that he was killed with a blunt instrument.'

'At least that's in the tradition.'

'I don't understand.'

'I'm sorry, I was being very English and covering up emotion with facetiousness. In England, people are murdered with blunt instruments, never hammers, iron bars, or coshes . . . I'm talking nonsense even before I've finished my first drink. The fact is, it's all been one hell of a shock. When he disappeared, I presumed that despite the evidence there'd been some sort of problem that would be sorted out – that's what I wanted to believe. Then I learned that he was dead . . . He's been the kind of friend not everyone's lucky enough to find. From the moment Mary

– my wife – was taken ill, he couldn't have done more to help. There were money problems because I'd used up all my savings . . . To find the bloodsuckers of today, one doesn't have to look any further than the medical profession. The only people who can knowingly overcharge because they're guaranteed an endless succession of customers . . . As you'll gather, I've a warped opinion of them all.' He drank.

'I think you've said that you knew Señor Cooper well?'

'Probably as well as it is possible. I've always held that everyone has a corner of his being which he never releases – perhaps even to himself.'

'Were you, in truth, aware that Señora Cooper was having an affair?'

Field said nothing.

'Did you know that Señora Cooper was very friendly with Señor Burns?'

'I heard you the first time but, ostrich-like, hoped that if I didn't answer, the question would go away. There's been a rumour. I've taken care not to try to find out if there's any justification for it.'

'Even though you were such a friend of the señor's, you didn't think you should tell him?'

'That dangerous myth, it's always best for truth to out. What was to be gained by telling him? If the rumour was false I'd be needlessly causing him great mental pain. If it was true, but he was in total and happy ignorance of the fact, why force him to face it before there was no other option? By their very nature, affairs tend to be temporary and so he might never have learned of his own accord. It's the knowing of the truth that hurts, not the truth itself.' He drained his glass, stood. 'Are you ready for a recharge?' He took Alvarez's glass, went inside.

When he returned, he handed one glass across, sat.

'Do you know Señor Burns?' Alvarez asked.

'I've never met him. Rachael has probably made certain of that, knowing how I feel about loyalty, marriage, and all those old-fashioned standards which so amuse the young of today. She was probably worried I'd say what I think. She needn't have worried. I suffer in full the Englishman's inability to be openly rude due to the dread of a scene.'

'Did you visit Ca'n Oliver yesterday?'

'I was there in the evening.'

'For any particular reason?'

'A flush of self-satisfied do-gooding. I thought Rachael might like company to help take her mind off the world for a while. But she wasn't in and so I left after checking the pool to make certain Jorge was keeping it clean. Neither of them has enough Spanish to deal with the staff.'

'Did you go into the house?'

'No.'

'Could you have done?'

'Not without getting a key from Rosa or Clara. Oliver only left me one when both he and Rachael were away. That wasn't because he didn't trust me – I hope! – but because he's that sort of a man.'

'Perhaps rather a subtle difference?'

Field smiled briefly. 'A man can be generally suspicious while specifically trusting.'

'Do you know what was the time when you were there?'

'Not with any accuracy. I suppose it was around half nine, judging by the fact that the light was beginning to mellow. All I can say for certain is that I was back here just before ten when I listened to the news on the radio.'

It was all said with such openness that it seemed Field failed completely to understand the possible significance of his answers. The naivety of innocence. Yet, Alvarez thought, knowing that little was ever done in the village or the countryside without someone's being aware of the fact, apparent naivety could be a clever ploy. He suddenly cursed his mind, made eternally suspicious by his job. The man who spent his life cleaning stables smelled dung even when he put a rose to his nose.

*　　　*　　　*

127

Serra was picking ripe tomatoes off plants that had been staked and whose side shoots had been nipped out, a system of cultivation that had only recently been accepted by the farmers who, despite the lower quality and lost fruit, had previously allowed the plants to grow unchecked and unstaked because that was how it had always been done.

Alvarez walked up to where Serra was working. 'That's some nice fruit.'

'And it's all going into market, even if you tell me it looks sweeter than a virgin's nipple.'

'You're so suspicious you'd demand to see Peter's ID card before you'd believe his halo's genuine.'

Serra picked the final two ripe tomatoes on the plant, straightened up. 'If you're not on the cadge, what do you want?'

'The answers to some questions.'

'I've no time for answers or questions.'

'You're going to have to find time. Señor Cooper was murdered last night.'

He half turned and shouted across to his wife. 'It's right what they've been saying. The English señor bastard has been murdered.'

'God rest his soul,' she said.

'There's no need for Him to bother Himself with that one!'

Alvarez said: 'Seems like he won't be able to stop you pinching his water any more.'

'It's him what's been doing the thieving. Using water on flowers and grass at this time of the year. The silly sod deserved to be murdered.'

'And you decided he'd get what he deserved?'

'Are you trying to say I did him in?'

'It was one way of getting your own back on him for making you look a fool.'

'Who says he did?' Serra demanded furiously.

'It's common knowledge he got the better of you, and him only a foreigner. There's some saying you've grown so soft, you'll soon be giving to charity.'

'Anyone talks like that in front of me and I'll smash his face.'

'Like you smashed the señor?'

'I ain't seen him since the last time he was belly-aching over the water.'

'Where were you yesterday evening?'

'Where d'you think? Working.'

'When did you leave here?'

'When the work was done.'

'Was that before dark?'

'And if it was?'

'How long before?'

'I don't have a watch and so don't waste my time looking at it.'

'You'd know the time near enough. And when the wind's right you can hear the church clock from here.'

'Maybe it was nine,' Serra shouted, annoyed by Alvarez's refusal to be annoyed.

'Did you go straight home?'

'No.'

'Where did you go?'

'To the bar.'

'How long were you there?'

'What's it to you?'

'I'll need to try to find someone who'll confirm where you were.'

'Haven't I just told you?' he shouted. 'You're so bloody stupid, you don't know how many algarroba beans make six.'

CHAPTER 17

Dolores said: 'Pass your plate, Enrique.'

Alvarez looked up. 'No more for me.'

'You don't like it?'

'I had so much the first helping.'

Her expression darkened. 'Perhaps you find my fabada tasteless?'

This time, he decided, he wasn't going to succumb to her emotional blackmail. Jaime might always weakly give in for the sake of a peaceful life, but he was made of sterner stuff. 'It's delicious, but I'm simply not . . .'

'You are so simple you think you can fool me!'

Jaime, Isabel and Juan watched and listened with intense interest.

'Not hungry? You are hungry! But not for my fabada.'

'What's that supposed to mean?'

'You know full well.'

Her manner as much as her words identified the real cause of her annoyance.

'For your information, I have not lost my appetite because I am yearning after some foreign blonde.'

Jaime spoke without thought. 'Is it the one who swims naked?'

'She does *what*?' demanded Dolores shrilly.

A friend's words could be more dangerous than an enemy's blows, Alvarez thought bitterly.

She put her hands on her hips. Her dark-brown eyes smouldered. 'You confess that you know a woman so lost to modesty that she swims without a costume?'

'Where does she go swimming?' Juan asked hopefully.

She swung round. 'Be quiet!'

Juan cowered back in the chair. Isabel pulled faces at him, silently jeering.

Dolores turned back. With all the fervour of an operatic diva approaching her death on a high C, she said: 'Has any other woman had to suffer men so depraved that they corrupt not only themselves, but their young? Has there been another woman so scorned and humiliated?'

The situation threatened to become heated and confused to the point where anything could happen. Alvarez said hurriedly: 'The only reason I've had any contact with the señora is through the case. It was not I who saw her swimming in the nude, it was the gardener. And she wouldn't look twice at me, since she had a husband and a boyfriend.'

'And you are so corrupted that you are willing to become her third victim?'

It had been Escanellas – that great pragmatist of the late nineteenth century – who'd written, Hold fast to your principles if certain they will not injure you.

'I'm too old to stand in a queue. And you know something? This fabada couldn't be equalled by the King's chef, and all the talking has given me fresh appetite.' He held out his plate.

Twelve buses were parked on the front of Cala Xima and the tourists they had brought filled the pavements and frequently spilled on to the road, forcing Alvarez to drive unusually slowly; even so, one couple engrossed in each other only escaped death because of his very quick reactions. Holidays befuddled the wits.

He parked in front of the Hotel Pedro and went into the air-conditioned foyer. The desk clerk remembered him and, despite his saying this was not necessary, called the assistant manager.

'All I want is a quick word with Señor White,' Alvarez said.

The assistant manager fiddled with his short right-hand sideburn, twisting the hair between thumb and forefinger.

'The trouble's a lot more serious than you suggested before, isn't it?'

'Did I suggest anything?'

'You claimed it was no more than a routine inquiry. Since you're from Llueso and there's been a report on the local radio of the murder of an Englishman there, I presume that's why you're here now. I wouldn't call a murder investigation a routine inquiry . . . Look, I'm not trying to find out exactly what's going on, but I do have to judge whether the hotel could be affected. If so, I'll need to warn the chairman of the company.'

'Nothing will happen today to cause any problems.'

'An ambiguous guarantee, Inspector! But if you could keep things as low key as possible? . . . I'll find out if Señor White is around.'

The assistant manager was gone for less than a couple of minutes. 'He's by the pool. I'll show you the way.'

The swimming pool was in the shape of an unequally proportioned figure of eight, the smaller circle shallow and the much larger one, deep; a bar was set into the side of the latter and swimmers could sit on stools in the water as they drank. Around the pool there were tables and chairs with sun umbrellas to give shade.

'Over to the right, halfway along.'

Alvarez looked across the pool. White, in multicoloured swimming trunks, was seated at one of the tables. The assistant manager smiled a professional *au revoir*, returned into the building.

As Alvarez approached, White looked up and his expression mirrored his sudden, sharp annoyance.

'Good afternoon, señor. I'm sorry to have to bother you again, but there are more questions I have to ask.'

'First, I've one for you. The American consulate says you've no right to hold my passport without just cause. What's the goddamn just cause?'

'Perhaps it would be better to discuss the matter somewhere less public?'

White hesitated, then stood, picked up the glass on the

132

table, and strode off towards the building. Alvarez followed, almost having to run to keep pace.

White settled in the corner of the large lounge in which were only four other people. Alvarez sat opposite him. A waiter came up and asked them what they would like. White tapped his glass, Alvarez, deciding the hotel would wish to prove its generosity once more, ordered a Carlos I.

As the waiter left, White said harshly: 'What's the answer?'

'Have you listened to the radio today?'

'No.'

'And none of the staff have mentioned the news?'

'Is this the sixty-four-dollar show? If you've something to say, say it.'

The American vice of rushing. They'd never understood that often haste meant waste. 'And you have not spoken by phone to anyone at Ca'n Oliver?'

'Maybe you'd like a full list of everything else I haven't done?'

'Then you will not know that Señor Cooper reappeared last night.'

White blanked his expression so that it was impossible to gauge how, or whether, the news affected him. The ability to hide his thoughts was one he shared with the Mallorquin peasant – a similarity, Alvarez decided with pleasure, he would not welcome.

'He's at his place, then?'

'In one sense, yes; in another, no.'

'Can't you say any goddamn thing straightforwardly?'

'His body was discovered early this morning. He had been murdered.'

White drank. He put the glass down. He said, neutralizing his tone so much that ironically it gained emphasis: 'How murdered?'

'He was struck on the head several times with something solid.'

'What something?'

133

'At the moment, that is unknown. The murderer took the weapon away with him.'

The waiter returned and put a coaster down on the table, a glass on the coaster, and was about to add the bill when Alvarez explained that the assistant manager would be responsible for it. Looking doubtful, the waiter left.

'Señor, when I last spoke to you, I said that Señor Cooper had disappeared and his car had been discovered in circumstances which made it seem he must have committed suicide. Yet there were certain facts which contradicted such a possibility. Now I know that he did not die then. So how to explain events? The only reasonable explanation that I have reached is that Señor Cooper wanted someone to believe him dead, but raising a presumption of suicide is not easy when there is no body; people in trouble often try to fake their own deaths. Murder, however, presents a different scenario. It is common for there to be no body for the simple reason that its absence is greatly to the advantage of the murderer, since without it there can often be no proof there has been a murder. So Señor Cooper, a man of talent, decided to set the scene for suicide, making certain that evidence must raise the probability that it was in fact a case of murder. Would one call that a double bluff? If this was the true position, one very important question has to be answered. What would make someone in Señor Cooper's position – wealthy, married to a beautiful wife – go to such lengths? It would have to be something that so frightened him he could think of no other way of escape. What was that something?'

'How the hell would I know?'

'He was due to have lunch at home, yet after your visit on the Sunday, the maid described him as having been in a very distressed state and he left the house without a word of explanation. It would seem obvious that it was the subject of your conversation that so terrified him.'

'We never got beyond small talk, British decorous style.'

'That bores, but never frightens.'

'Sure. So nothing I said frightened him.'

'Why did you visit him?'

'You need to be told everything six times? Friends back in the States suggested I look him up because he'd be glad to meet me. They couldn't have been more wrong.'

'You'd no other reason?'

'None.'

'Then why did you previously visit the area and study the señor's house through binoculars?'

'I told you before, that's all crap.'

Alvarez sighed. He raised his glass and drained the last of the smooth, rich brandy. 'Where were you last night between nine and ten?'

White said contemptuously: 'You think I killed the limey?'

'It's possible.'

'Like an honest politician is possible. Between nine and ten I was in the restaurant here. The meat was so tough, I sent it back with the suggestion the chef use it to resole his shoes. He'll likely remember that.'

'I should imagine he would.'

'So you can return my passport.'

'Not before I've heard from America as to whether or not you have any known criminal connections.' Alvarez stood. 'Thank you for your help, señor.'

'If there's one thing I hate, it's a goddamn polite cop,' White said violently, for once not bothering to mask his emotions.

CHAPTER 18

When Alvarez entered the small office in the boatyard, Delgado was swearing over the phone, using to the full the rich, colourful, sacrilegious obscenity with which the Mallorquin language was endowed. He slammed the receiver down. 'What do you want?'

'I wouldn't mind a friendly welcome.'

He delivered his opinion of friendly welcomes.

'All right, let's move on. I need to talk to Señor Burns.'

'Then why waste my time?'

'Since he works here . . .'

'Works here, does he? That's news to me! Rings up after lunch and says he's suddenly been taken ill and is in bed. You can't rely on a foreigner even to stay healthy.'

Alvarez left and drove the short distance to the flat. The old woman was seated in the shade and he greeted her. She moved her head from side to side, mumbled something he failed to understand, and gesticulated with one hand. A bad day, he thought with sympathy as he climbed the outside stairs to Burns's flat.

He was about to knock on the door when he reasoned that if Burns were ill in bed, it would be kinder, if possible, not to make him have to come to the door. He turned the handle and pushed, found the door was unlocked, stepped inside and called out.

'Who the bloody hell is it?' Burns demanded.

'Inspector Alvarez.'

'What d'you want?'

'A word.'

'I'm too ill.'

'Then I'm afraid I'll have to come through . . .'

'I'll be out.'

When Burns entered from the inner room, dressed in T-shirt and shorts, he appeared more belligerent than ill. 'What gives you the right to come bursting in here?'

'The door was unlocked. And since Señor Delgado told me you were too ill to work, I judged it kinder to enter, if that were possible, than to cause you to have to come to the door.'

'Next time, try knocking.'

'It would seem you have recovered.'

'I still feel as if something were gnawing away at my guts.'

'Then let us sit down.'

'Let you clear off and come back when I'm feeling better.'

'I certainly would like to, but for the moment that is impossible.'

Burns sat.

'I am sure you will have heard that Señor Cooper has been found dead?' Alvarez said, after removing a pile of yachting magazines from the second chair.

'He's been dead for days.'

'He has been missing, presumed dead. He was killed last night.'

'All very dramatic, but what's that to do with me?'

'You knew him.'

'Knowing him consisted of meeting him once at his place and not being offered a drink.'

'But you know Señora Cooper well?'

'And that gets your twisted mind all excited? We ran a course and when it was over, we said goodbye. So that's the end of it.'

'I would like to accept that, but for the moment cannot be so certain that your relationship with the señora is of no importance to my investigation.'

'I'm telling you . . .'

'When you and the señora were together, she could have said something that seemed inconsequential at the time, but may be of importance now when I have to try to find out who murdered the señor. Did she ever mention a Señor White?'

'No.'

'Did she ever say that the señor had been or was thinking of going to America?'

'No.'

'Has she spoken about the trouble the señor had with his neighbour over water rights?'

'Just that the stupid old fool next door was forever causing hassle and they were having to employ a solicitor to make him see sense.'

'When did you last see the señora?'

'What's it to you?'

'I have to know.'

After a moment, Burns said sullenly: 'Like I've told you before, it was some good time ago. Before her husband vanished.'

'Where were you last night, between nine and ten?'

'Eating.'

'Where?'

'At the Celler Verde.'

'That is not here?'

'Santa Maria.'

'It is a fair way to go for a meal.'

'So is there a law against travelling?'

'Were you on your own?'

Burns hesitated. 'No,' he finally said.

'Who were you with?'

'A woman.'

'Señora Cooper?'

'Haven't I just said I've not seen her recently? I picked up a woman on the beach and she turned out to be a culture vulture and wanted to see the real Mallorca. So I took her to the celler and she loved the bare tables, trestles, wine casks and jugs of wine, and thought she'd been on safari.'

'I shall, of course, have to establish that your companion

138

was not the señora and so I will be questioning the staff and, if necessary, showing them a photo of her.'

Burns swore.

'Do you not understand that when a man has been murdered, I have to establish the motive for his murder? So I ask myself, suppose the affair between you and the señora had not come to an end and the señor had learned about it, what might have happened? I think that he was not a man with a generous heart, ready to forgive. He would have determined to do whatever most hurt his wife and, indirectly, you. And the easiest way of attaining that goal must be to change his will and leave her nothing, instead of everything. That frightened the señora because without the wealth how could she be certain to hold you? So she persuaded you to kill him before he could actually change his will . . .'

'No!' Rachael cried.

They turned to see her in the doorway of the inner room. She was wearing a hand-embroidered silk blouse and an iridescent skirt and the shaft of sunlight that came through the window created a texture of light at the back of the room that touched her, as she stood with one hand to her throat, with a hint of ethereality.

She moved forward, to become purely physical. She faced Alvarez, said in a small, husky voice: 'How could you even imagine such beastly things?'

'Sadly, it is my job to do so,' he replied defensively.

'But to suggest I'd want to hurt Oliver and would ask Neil . . .' She swung round. 'Tell him you wouldn't ever have hurt Oliver, not in a thousand years, not for all the treasures of the world.'

'If he thinks I'm a murderer, he's a bloody fool,' Burns said violently.

She spoke to Alvarez once more. 'You see?'

'Unfortunately, señora, I know that he is a liar.'

'Because he told you he hadn't seen me in days and days and that it was someone else he took to the restaurant? He only did that to defend me. Don't you understand what the local community would say if they ever learned? They rush to think the worst. It would give them enough to gossip about for weeks and they'd call me a complete bitch, having an affair when my husband was missing and probably dead.'

'But you were . . .'

'You think that because I was out with Neil last night and I'm here now . . . You're just like all the others. And I thought you were so different because you seemed so kind and understanding . . . Just how wrong can one be?'

'Señora, what am I to believe when I come here this afternoon and find you in the bedroom?'

She sat on the bedraggled settee, rested her elbows on her knees, cupped her chin on her hands, stared into space. 'Because we knew it was summer madness, we also knew it had to have an end. When it finished, we agreed not to see each other again. But then Oliver disappeared and I didn't know how to live through the agony because I loved him so.' Her voice briefly rose. 'I loved him, despite what had happened. You've got to understand that.' She once more spoke quietly. 'The world seemed to be crushing me until I also wanted to commit suicide to bring everything to an end. Then Neil rang to say how sorry he was to hear what had happened and I begged him to take me out somewhere so that just for a short while I could escape. At first, he wouldn't. He said that in the circumstances it was impossible. I went on and on, begging him; I even said he owed it to me because of what happened before. I'm not proud of that. It was a filthy thing to do, to blackmail him emotionally. But I was so desperate . . . In the end, he agreed. We had a meal in Santa Maria because we were as certain as we could be that no one else from Llueso would be there to see us. And being with him, realizing that the rest of the world was still alive, made such a difference.

'Then I returned home and found Oliver, lying in the dressing-room, his head a terrible sight. It was like being put on the rack. Even though I knew he had to be dead, I tried to will him alive . . . The doctor came and wanted to give me a sedative, but I wouldn't take it. I can remember thinking that since Oliver had suffered so much, I had to suffer as well . . . I was slightly crazy. But one corner of my mind remained clear enough to know that I had to pull myself together and that Neil could help me do that. So I phoned him. And because he's someone who can really care, he told me to come here. With him, some of the blackness began to slip away. But you think . . . you think he and I . . .'

'Señora, I have to say it again, when I arrived, you were both in the bedroom.'

She raised her head, lowered her hands, faced him. 'We were in this room when Neil happened to look out through the window and see you approaching. He said that if you found me here, you'd draw the wrong conclusion. I argued that you weren't that kind of person and you'd understand, but he insisted we hide in the bedroom and make it seem the flat was empty, so you'd go away . . . Only you didn't. And now I know I was so wrong about you. You're just as ready to think the worst.'

He would have given much to accept all she'd said, but duty drove him to say: 'You arrived back at Ca'n Oliver early this morning to find your husband's body. Where were you during the night and until six this morning?'

'You think I'm still lying? You really can believe I'd spend the night with Neil when my husband was missing?'

'It doesn't matter what I think, I have to determine the facts.'

'Then I'm going to have to disappoint you once again. Neil was driving me home from the restaurant when I told him I couldn't face spending the night on my own so I asked him to take me to Muriel's. She put me up for the night, but I couldn't sleep and in the end decided that since I'd have to face life sooner or later, it might as well be sooner. I wrote a note to explain and left it on the kitchen table, walked home. Which was when I found . . .' She buried her face in her hands.

'Satisfied?' Burns demanded angrily.

'Señor, sometimes one has a duty to perform . . .'

'Which you've performed in hobnail boots. Why don't you clear out?'

He left.

Alvarez replaced the receiver. The owner of Celler Verde remembered the two foreigners, each of whom he'd personally served with tortilla, lomo con col, and Xulla del cel; he remembered them first because the celler was not frequented by many foreigners, secondly because the man had spoken in Spanish. He was hazy when it came to describing the man, but the woman . . . He'd have one like her on each arm after he'd won six hundred million on the lottery and persuaded his wife to see her cousins in Salamanca.

Alvarez said that he might be asked to identify two photographs, thanked him, rang off. Even without photographic identification, there could be little doubt that it had been Rachael and Burns who had eaten at Celler Verde. So they also had an alibi . . .

He was going to have to phone the superior chief. He sighed, reached down and pulled open the bottom right-hand drawer of the desk, brought out the bottle of brandy and a glass. He had a generous drink, decided that in the circumstances he needed another.

Salas's greeting was typical. 'What is it?'

'I have to report, señor, that I have now questioned all those whom I identified as having a motive for Señor Cooper's murder.'

'And?'

'Each person has an alibi for the presumed time of death.'

'Does that lead you to any conclusion?'

'Obviously, none of them can be the murderer.'

'Your perspicacity is unusually sharp.'

'There is the one further possible suspect, whom I've mentioned before. Señor Field knew Señor Cooper well, does not have an alibi, and was at Ca'n Oliver during the evening. One of the maids saw him drive away, but can't place the time; he admits to having returned home to arrive a little before ten.'

'You refer to him as a possible suspect. With all the evidence to hand, you see no reason to regard him as the prime suspect?'

'As I believe I mentioned, not only does he lack any motive, his relationship with the dead man argues against his having murdered him. Señor Cooper had helped him financially when his wife was seriously ill and that naturally left him deeply grateful. He spoke to me about these feelings and I have no doubt that he was telling me the truth. Beyond that, he possesses a tremendous desire to succeed as a painter – a desire that in some rather obscure way is fuelled by the memory of his wife – and Señor Cooper, who was in a position to do so, was giving him all possible help. Señor Cooper's death brings that help to an end and, I think, makes it very unlikely he will ever become a true artist, which will leave his ambition, with its deeper meaning, unfulfilled.'

'If he is an artist, he is probably a pervert. Examine closely the relationship between the two men.'

And he had been accused of gratuitously introducing libidinous details into cases! 'I would think it very unlikely that Señor Cooper was of such persuasion. He is married to a woman . . .'

'Why must you always argue? Learn to do as you're ordered, without comment.'

'Yes, señor.'

'Did you tell me that the house has a good security system?'

'It's very good.'

'But no alarm sounded?'

'That's right.'

'And there's no sign of a forced entry?'

'That is so.'

'Then has it occurred to you that the murderer must be acquainted with all the details of the security system?'

'Indeed. Which is one reason why it seemed Señor Burns

and Señora Cooper were the most likely suspects. But both of them have an alibi.'

'What about this artist fellow, who was at the house around the time of the murder?'

'Whenever the Coopers were away, he kept an eye on the property and for that reason was given a key to the house; so, of course, he has a full knowledge of the security system. But according to him, when they returned from their holiday, Señor Cooper always reclaimed the key. On Wednesday evening, he says he went to see if he could help the señora. She was not there, so he didn't enter the house.'

'What stopped his having made an impression of the key when he had been given it?'

'Nothing. Only . . .'

'Well?'

'With no motive for murdering the señor, for motive to wish him to continue to live as long as possible, I find it very difficult to conceive that he can be the murderer.'

'All the more reason for considering it as highly probable . . . Why did Cooper originally fake his own death?'

'It surely has to be because of what happened during Señor White's visit.'

'What *did* happen?'

'I haven't been able to discover that.'

'Having taken the trouble to fake his death, why did he return to his house?'

'I haven't identified the reason yet.'

'What is the connection between his faked death and his murder?'

'There's no apparent connection. But it has to be too much of a coincidence . . .'

'Since Cooper has done everything to hide himself and did not even alert his wife to his return, how could the murderer have known he was in the house?'

'That does seem to raise a difficulty . . .'

'Even allowing for the fact that it is your investigation,

I am astounded to be met with such a catalogue of unresolved questions.'

'It is early days . . .'

'I am tempted to point out that whenever you are concerned, it is perpetual night.'

'I know it looks rather confused at the moment, but I do have the feeling that –' The line went dead.

He poured himself a third brandy. He should have remembered that the superior chief had an irrational dislike of 'feelings'. What he had been going to say was that he had the feeling there was one central pivot to this case and once that was identified, all the questions would be answered. He would not have added that at the moment he had not the slightest idea, not even a 'feeling', as to what the pivot could be.

CHAPTER 19

Something obviously was wrong. Having called him once, Dolores had forgotten to do so a second and third time and so now he was going to be late for work. And although she had remembered to go out and buy a couple of ensaimadas for his breakfast, she had not made him hot chocolate until he'd reminded her. He surreptitiously studied her, wondering how seriously life would be disrupted if by some malignant chance she were ill . . .

'You'll have to say something to him,' she said suddenly and violently.

He'd been about to eat a piece of ensaimada. He held it in front of his mouth as he waited.

'How can I have married such a man. At his age!'

The anger, the bewilderment, the hint of helplessness, led him to the obvious conclusion. Curiosity made him consider the possibilities. Bárbara? Leonor?

'He'll have a heart attack.'

That, surely, was the happiest of ways to die.

'He'll be beaten black and blue.'

Sado-masochism?

'He'll drink himself incapable.'

He tried to offer her some slight consolation. 'That might not be such a bad thing.'

'How can you speak such stupidity?'

He was taken aback by her fierce response. 'Well, it's like this – if he drinks too much, he won't be able to . . . you know.'

'I do not know.'

'At his age, drinking too much makes it impossible. And that'll bring the affair to a sudden end.'

146

'Mother of God, you are telling me that Jaime has become mixed up with another woman?'

'It's you who's said he is.'

'Puta!' she shouted. 'I'll name her dishonour in every street. Who is she?'

Jaime stepped into the kitchen and, as always failing to discern in time what was the prevailing atmosphere, said belligerently: 'What the hell's all the noise about?'

'Do you, then, expect me to whisper?' she demanded.

'No, but there's no need to shout.'

'You think there is no fire in my belly?' She dropped her voice and spoke with all the hissing venom of a striking mamba. 'There is fire enough for me to rip off your cojones so that a woman has only to look at you to laugh!'

Jaime said wildly to Alvarez: 'What the hell have you been telling her?'

'Only trying to point out that if you are mixed up with another woman and drink too much . . .'

'Me with another woman?'

'Who is she?' she demanded.

'I don't know why you're going on like this.'

'If I find out you're lying . . .'

'For God's sake, you've said what you'd do. I swear I've not so much as looked at anyone else.'

She stared at Alvarez through lowered lids. 'You told me he had a woman.'

'I thought that was what you were telling me.'

'I said he is to be a Moor.'

Language could complicate far more easily than it could explain. 'Look, I'm sorry, but I misunderstood what you were talking about. That's why I said . . .'

'Bloody fools like you should learn to keep your mouths shut,' Jaime said bitterly.

She placed her hands on her hips. 'You are pleased to call Enrique a bloody fool? You are twice the bloody fool he could ever be. It is not he who agrees to be a Moor; who will visit every bar in the village because the drinks will be free; who will end up a sodden, incapable wreck.'

She paused. 'Men!' she shouted, making them start. 'When God made Adam, He made a terrible mistake.' She lowered her hands, marched out of the kitchen.

'And you've made my day,' Jaime muttered.

'How was I to know she was on about you being a Moor for the fiesta? From the way she was worrying, I thought you'd found yourself a nymphomaniac.'

'In Llueso? You're even dafter than I thought.' His tone was angry, resentful, and a shade regretful.

A résumé of the postmortem report was telephoned through soon after ten.

The victim had died from a series of blows to the head which had fractured the skull, due to its inherent weakness (bearing out Dr Pons's judgement), and caused serious intracranial haemorrhage. It was possible that the victim had suffered a period of unconsciousness before death intervened; it was even conceivable that he had briefly regained consciousness (there were well-documented cases where this had happened).

The many blows had been delivered by an assailant facing the victim; the blows had been continued as the victim fell and at least a couple had been delivered once he was on the ground, suggesting either a grim determination or a measure of loss of self-control. It was probable that the weapon had not been of a very substantial nature and had in part or whole been made of wood (a sliver of varnished wood had been embedded in one of the wounds; this had been sent to the laboratory for further investigation, but it was doubtful that anything of importance would be determined from it).

The assailant would have been stained with the victim's blood and, probably, body tissue.

After the call was over, Alvarez considered what he had just learned. Not all that much. But at least he could now be certain that the murderer had taken the weapon away with him.

*   *   *

The phone rang as he was wondering whether Dolores would have pulled herself together sufficiently to prepare a decent lunch.

'My name's Gore,' a man said in English.

'Yes, señor?'

'I've been wondering whether to phone. I mean, I may be drawing a long bow, if you know what I mean?'

'If you will give me the details, señor, I shall be able to judge.'

'Yes, of course. Only . . . To be perfectly frank, I'd prefer it if people didn't learn what I'm going to tell you. They'd start to think, especially as we've had to stop employing our daily because she demanded a thousand two hundred an hour. That's a lot of money; more than they'd pay at home. When we first came here, it was forty an hour and that was being generous. Everything's changed so. I can remember . . .'

'What have you to tell me?'

'The fact is, I borrowed money. If they learned that, some of the people we know would start to think we've run into serious financial problems and would begin to cold-shoulder us.'

'You borrowed money from whom?'

'Mark this, it was only to help over a rough patch. Our son was made redundant and what with the new baby, things became very difficult for him so we gave him all our reserve cash. Then one of the firms in which I'd a lot of shares went bust and that capital's been lost. It was weighing on my mind so much that I found myself telling him about it. Usually keep such things to myself, of course; not done to bother others with these matters. Had a few and that didn't help. Anyway, he offered to lend me some money.'

'Who are you talking about?'

'Oliver Cooper. Didn't I say?'

'No, señor, you didn't,' Alvarez replied, suddenly interested in what was being said.

'I refused. Neither a lender nor a borrower be, if your

friend you wish to see. But Oliver said it wouldn't be an interest-free loan, it would be a commercial one. I still didn't want to touch it, but the good lady wife said I was being stupid because it would be no different from borrowing from a bank. And we did have to find some extra money to tide us over if we were to maintain our social position.'

'How much did you borrow?'

'Two thousand pounds.'

'And why exactly are you telling me this?'

'Because of what happened when he gave me the cheque. He looked at me as if . . . As if he were sneering at me because having to borrow made me so much less of a man than he. So what I've been wondering since I heard about the terrible murder is if he lent someone else money and they realized he was jeering at them and this made them so angry they killed him . . . I just thought I ought to tell you.'

Amateur psychologists so often blossomed in murder cases. Trying to sound grateful, Alvarez said: 'Thank you, señor.'

'Just wanted to help. He wasn't the friendliest of men, but murder's murder . . . By the way, to whom will I have to repay the money?'

'Whoever inherits the estate.'

'That'll be Rachael. But as I told him when he phoned and wanted the money then and there, it's going to take time to repay it all because it's got to come out of future income. But repay it all I will, no one need think twice on that score.'

'When did he phone you to ask for repayment?'

'Wednesday. When he said who he was, I told him he could quote Mark Twain. Didn't understand what I meant, but then he sounded in one hell of a rush and in a very emotional state. Not surprising, really. I tried to ask him what had happened, of course, but all he'd say was that there'd been a terrible mistake.'

'Can you say what the time was when he phoned you?'

'A couple of minutes before eleven. Which made it really rather ridiculous to think I could find two thousand, plus interest, at that time of night.'

'Eleven at night?'

'That's right.'

'Impossible!'

'But I can be quite certain. We always go to bed reasonably early and there was a film starting at eleven so I was waiting to start recording it – I've never mastered how to work time-record. They say that people of my age seldom do because we haven't a gismo intelligence. So when the phone rang and there were only a couple of minutes to go, and the lady wife was already upstairs, I started the recording. It turned out to be rather a stupid film.'

'You are quite certain the caller was Señor Cooper?'

'Not a shadow of doubt. Recognized the voice immediately. Added to which, who else could know I'd borrowed the two thousand from him?'

Cooper had been alive at least one and a half hours later than the time at which he had, until now, been presumed to have died . . .

'I thought I had to tell you about the way he'd behaved, despite *de mortuis nil nisi bonum* and all that. One owes a greater duty to justice than to one's friends. Wouldn't you agree?'

Gore's conscience needed reassurance. 'Señor, that is absolutely correct. It was very right of you to tell me this.'

'I'm so glad of that. It's difficult, but there are times when one has to forget the injunction against sneaking.'

Only the English could, in the course of a murder investigation, concern themselves with the ethics of sneaking. The Spanish, along with most continentals, were brought up on the art of denouncing. Alvarez made a note of Gore's address, thanked him for his help, rang off.

It was ironic that Gore believed his evidence about Cooper's attitude was material, while that concerning the timing of the phone call was totally irrelevant . . .

Get but one figure in a complicated mathematical calculation wrong and the result had to be incorrect. Work to the wrong time of death and the investigation had at best to be flawed, at worst, useless. When Salas heard about this, he would talk about crass, arrant, gross incompetence. But it wasn't really. He'd always worked to the best information available. Dr Pons had estimated the time of death at between nine and twelve. Because the smashed watch had shown 9.23, it had been logical to accept the further judgement that this marked the actual time when the injuries had been inflicted. Now he knew that death had not taken place then, he had to accept that all the alibis for 9.23 were immaterial . . . Or were they? The assistant at the Institute of Forensic Anatomy had mentioned the possibility that death had followed unconsciousness. Could the blows have been struck at 9.23 and the assailant, not intending death – as the medical evidence surely could suggest? – have left, believing Cooper would recover? Then he indeed had recovered consciousness, only to die some time after 11.00? Yet unless dazed beyond all reason, he would have called for help. And if that dazed, he must have sounded confused when he'd telephoned Gore which clearly he had not; indeed, was it really conceivable that in such circumstances his overriding concern would be to have demanded that his loan be repaid?

He was completely missing something. Something, he was certain, that had raised half a question in his mind at the time, but had then been forgotten because it had been only half . . . The watch glass! What was the make of watch? One of the luxury ones . . . Rolex? Audemars-Piguet? . . . Cotti.

He rang Inquiries, who automatically refused to search out the telephone number of Cotti's headquarters in Switzerland until he said it was police work.

The PRO at Cotti spoke near-perfect English. He said, with smooth, irritating Swiss superiority, that the glass used in the company's watches was of the most superior quality and would never shatter if a person fell.

'But it might have been a defective glass?' he unwisely suggested.

He had to listen to a long lecture on quality control.

After the call was over, he assembled his thoughts. The watch had not marked the time when Cooper had been struck down. The glass had been smashed in order to suggest the wrong time of death, thereby enabling the murderer to create an alibi. Field had had no alibi, to fake so elaborate a one was surely beyond Serra's wit (and how could he have known Cooper was alive and in the house?). So only Rachael and Burns, and White, remained as suspects.

CHAPTER 20

White, seated by the hotel pool, was in the company of a younger woman whose charms were obvious.

White's expression changed. 'Don't you ever go on holiday?'

'Not very often,' Alvarez replied. 'My superior chief does not believe in them.'

'Your superior is going to get a goddamn earful from me.'

'Please do not restrain yourself on my account ... I would be grateful if I might speak to you.'

'Did I ever tell you what I think of polite cops?'

The woman said: 'Hon, shall I wander off and see if I can buy a paper?'

'Sure.'

She stood, walked away, expected and received considerable attention.

'Make it fast and make it short,' White said.

'Where were you on Wednesday night ... ?'

'Not again? Do you lot have to be told everything five times for it to climb into your register? I was in the restaurant here, trying to eat a piece of meat that back home would make a dog sue.'

'If you will let me finish?' Alvarez sat on the chair the woman had vacated and which was in the shade of the sun umbrella.

'So finish.'

'Where were you on Wednesday evening between eleven o'clock and midnight?'

'What's it to you?'

'Señor Cooper was murdered during that time.'

'When you were last here, it was nine thirty.'

'That is true.'

'So soon it'll be Thursday midday? Ever thought of joining the Keystone Kops?'

'I'm afraid I don't understand.'

White emptied his glass, replaced it on the table.

'Will you please tell me where you were between eleven and midnight, señor?'

'Dancing.'

'Where?'

'Here, to a band with left arms. Doesn't anyone on this island know what music is?'

'Were you with the señorita who was here a moment ago?'

'No.'

'Who were you with?'

'Her name's Helen.'

'And her surname?'

'How would I know? You think we flash visiting cards?'

'I shall have to speak to her, so perhaps you can help me identify her further?'

'Room seven-one-two.'

'Thank you.'

'Suppose I say I hate polite foreign cops so much my right arm's twitching?'

'Then perhaps I should point out that although some Spanish jails are quite salubrious these days, others have not changed.'

'I want my goddamn passport back.'

'As soon as I have heard from America, perhaps it will be possible for me to return it to you.'

'I've told the consul in Palma to get on to the ambassador in Madrid.'

'Then no doubt I shall be hearing from my superior chief belong long, but I think that for once he will agree with me and say that until we have heard from America, it must remain in our possession.' As he stood, he was convinced that although White's expression remained coolly blank, an inner anger was – as he had suggested earlier – urging him to violent action.

Once in the foyer, Alvarez crossed to the reception desk and asked for the name of the occupant of room 712. The clerk checked, said: 'Señorita Helen Hamill.'

'Would you page her, please? I'll be in the lounge.'

The lounge was as empty as it had been on previous occasions. A waiter asked him if he wanted anything. Despite the fact that he judged it wiser not to expect the hotel to pay yet again, he could not resist ordering a brandy.

A tall woman in her early twenties, with an open, attractive face, wearing a modestly cut, colourful cotton dress, stepped into the lounge and looked about her. Alvarez stood and said: 'Señorita Hamill?' She crossed the short distance to his table, moving with the easy rhythm of an athlete. Laughter, warmth, and honest friendship, he thought. Small wonder that White had not remained her companion.

'Who are you?' she asked, with the directness he had expected. She spoke English with the accent of windy moors.

He introduced himself. As they sat, the waiter returned. He asked if she'd like a drink, she shook her head.

'Why do you want to question me?' she asked, curious rather than apprehensive.

'Señorita, I need to ask you questions concerning another guest at this hotel. Please understand that this doesn't mean there is reason to believe he has done anything wrong, it is merely that I need to substantiate what he has told me.'

'Are you referring to Ernest?'

'Señor White, yes. He has told me that he was dancing with you on Wednesday evening.'

'That's right.'

'Can you say from when to when?'

'The dance was after dinner. I don't know exactly, but I imagine it started about half past ten. Madge and I were at our table and soon after the music started, Ernest came across and asked me to dance.'

'Madge is a friend?'

'We're on holiday together. We're friends of old and coincidentally we'd both reason to get away from it all . . .' Her gaze became unfocused.

He wondered if emotional problems were the reason?

She jerked her attention back to the present. 'Anyway, as I've said, he asked me to dance. Someone else spoke to Madge and we formed a foursome for the rest of the evening.'

'Roughly when did that finish?'

'It was around two o'clock.'

'And just to confirm things, from ten thirty until two, Señor White was with you?'

'That's right.'

'Thank you, señorita.'

She faced him, her blue eyes fixed on his. She said, with typical directness: 'I don't believe you've asked those questions just to check what he told you, so why have you?'

'I can assure you that that is the truth.'

'But not the whole truth. And it has to be because of something important.'

'That is so.'

'What?'

'A man has been killed and I am trying to discover who killed him. I now know that it cannot have been Señor White.'

'I see.' She hesitated, then said: 'Are you surprised?'

He didn't know how to answer that.

'I shouldn't have asked, should I? Only . . .'

'Yes, señorita?'

'You won't tell him, will you, but there's something about him . . . He was very amusing and very attentive; it was a great evening and I forgot all my worries. But afterwards he made it clear he was looking for further entertainment and when I put the stopper on that idea, he became all cold and angry. I suddenly had the feeling that he could be dangerous when he didn't get what he wanted.'

'However near the truth you may be, señorita, what you have just told me makes it quite certain that he did not commit the murder.'

Burns's greeting was no more welcoming than White's had been. He shook hands with the man to whom he'd been talking, walked around the stern of a yacht on a cradle, and came to a halt squarely in front of Alvarez. 'What the bloody hell is it this time? The Christian names of my great-grandparents?'

'Where were you from eleven o'clock onwards on Wednesday night?'

'It's beginning to sound as if there's been another Spanish cock-up.'

'If you will answer.'

Burns jammed his hands into the pockets of his stained overalls. 'Rachael told you.'

'She answered a different question.'

'I drove Rachael to Muriel's place.'

'Did you enter the house?'

'For once, Muriel was in a friendly, not a bitchy, mood – she'd been at the Crafters earlier on and they always lash out the booze to prove how generous they are, so I've been told.'

'When did you leave?'

'It was well after one.'

'Did you return to your flat?'

'Yeah.'

'Did anyone see you return?'

'How would I know?'

'Thank you, señor.'

'So next time you appear out of the woodwork, what'll it be; where was I this time last year?'

There were similarities between Burns and White, though neither man would have welcomed the comparison.

CHAPTER 21

In the summer, the main road between the port and Llueso was one of the most dangerous on the island; much of it was dead straight, speeds were high, and drivers' machismo flourished. But self-preservation was not the only reason for Alvarez's eschewing it whenever possible; due to the planner's belief that a straggling line of commercial premises made for attractive scenery, in many places the road was lined by ugly, sprawling complexes. In sharp contrast, the back roads went through countryside that remained countryside and open fields, crops, trees, and farm animals, provided the sense of continuity he was always seeking. There was no prior intention, then, to visit Field, but when he approached the lane which led down to the caseta, he slowed. It was still relatively early. If he continued on to the village, he would in all conscience have to return to the office. Who knew what work might be waiting there? He turned.

As he continued along the twisting lane in second gear, ready to brake sharply if he met any oncoming vehicle, since for most of the time there was not the room for passing, he mentally reviewed the facts. Initially, he had considered Field an unlikely suspect, since not only did he lack motive (there were motiveless murders, but he was convinced this was not one of them), he had had a direct interest in Cooper's continuing to live. When it had seemed that the watch marked the time of death, Field had been the only one without an alibi, but this still hadn't been sufficient definitely to point the finger of guilt at him. Now it was known that death had occurred at least one hour and forty minutes after the time the watch had stopped.

An attempt to provide an alibi by setting the hands of the watch back and then smashing it? If so, Field was cleared. Only if the assault had taken place at 9.23 and death much later, did that conclusion break down. And the arguments against that theory were strong.

He turned off the lane and drove to the caseta, parking by the side of the Seat 127. As he stepped out of his Ibiza, Field came round the corner of the building. 'I congratulate you on the timing. I've just taken out the ice from the fridge to go with the brandy.'

Politeness dictated that Alvarez dismiss the assumption that he should be offered a drink simply because he had arrived at an opportune moment: he considered hypocrisy to be one of the deadliest of sins. 'Then I'm glad that I neither hurried nor lingered.'

'Come on round. We'll sit inside, if that's all right with you? The mosquitoes are hungrier than ever and they've driven me inside every evening for days now.'

They walked round and into the caseta. There was no ceiling, as such, only the underside of the sloping roof, but the wooden beams were in good order and had been stained and the flat under-tiles (which had replaced the original bamboo) had been plastered; the walls were smooth and painted white, the floor was attractively tiled. The furniture was Mallorquin, simple but practical in design. A pedestal fan was turning at full speed, making a low, slashing hum.

'I'm afraid this place isn't palatial,' Field said, as he crossed to the television set and switched it off. 'But I pride myself that it's very much more in harmony with its surroundings than many of the houses that foreigners have had built. Carbuncles, one local builder calls them.'

'It is an apt description.' Alvarez looked around him. On one wall hung a painting that was a burst of colour and swirling forms. 'That is your work?' he asked admiringly.

'I painted it, but it's another copy. Like Oliver, I'm prepared to accept a copy when I cannot have the original. I've always thought that when Van Gogh was in the asylums at Arles and S. Remy, madness touched his work with something even beyond genius. For me, it also has a hidden value. I painted that after Mary died and I couldn't think of any reason for continuing to live; somehow it persuaded me I had a reason, even if I couldn't identify what that was. I brought it out because it reminds me of the battle I fought and, I think, won.'

'Then for you it must be more valuable than if it were the original.'

'I'm not surprised you understand.'

'Do you have any of your original paintings here?'

'Only one and that's damaged, which is why it's here. All the others are in England, looking for buyers – and very unlikely to find them now that Oliver's not around to push.'

'His death has been a double loss to you.'

'Yes, it has been. But I think it's reconciled me to the fact that I'll never become a second Grandma Moses. And by my age, ambition's really a scorpion, not a siren. The only thing is, I'll never justify Mary's faith in me. But perhaps in an afterlife one can be completely happy to see people as they really are, however they are; if that's so, she'll understand and approve.'

'I wonder if I might see the one painting of yours that you have?'

'Curious to judge how badly a good copyist can paint?'

Alvarez was sufficiently well acquainted with the English character to recognize the habit of self-deprecation when emotions were involved. 'Since, as I told you, I am totally ignorant about art, I shall only know if I do or don't like it.'

Field chuckled. 'The perfect critic for the amateur! And in the face of such perfection, I'm prepared to bare all.' He crossed to the far room and went through, to return with a canvas which he unrolled. An olive tree, gnarled and twisted, stood to the right of an abandoned rock-built shed. Hills, ranging back to distant mountains with jagged crests, formed the backdrop, cut off at the right-hand corner where the canvas had been torn.

It was an attractive painting, Alvarez thought, but offered no more than did dozens of other paintings he had seen in local exhibitions. But however ignorant of art, he did know enough about artists to understand that even when they asked for an honest opinion, that was the last thing they wanted. 'I think that's really good.' Hypocrisy might be a sin, but sins were necessary in the real world.

'For those sweet words, I'll pour doubles.' He rolled up the canvas, slipped it just inside the doorway of the far room. 'I mentioned coñac, but if you'd rather, there's gin, vodka, or wine?'

'Coñac, thank you.'

It was considerably later when Alvarez reluctantly brought the conversation round to the reason for his visit. 'I'm afraid I have to ask more questions.'

'No problem. But first, let me refill your glass.'

His drink refreshed, Alvarez said: 'We now know that the time of Señor Cooper's death was after eleven on Wednesday evening, not earlier. So I have to ask people where they were then, to confirm that they could not have been responsible for his death.'

'Or to confirm that they could . . . So where was I? Probably here, watching a film on satellite and wondering why so much money is wasted by so many people on so much bilge . . . Hang on. Late Wednesday evening? I was with the Calvo family, down the road.'

'Francisco Calvo?'

'You know him, then?'

'His wife, Marta, is a very distant cousin.'

'A wonderful old boy. Though I shouldn't be calling him old. Sometimes when I hear the English criticizing the Mallorquins, I feel the urge to introduce them to Francisco. Never do, of course. They'd be careful not to recognize that he's worth two of them any day of the week.'

*   *   *

Calvo stood in the doorway of his house. 'I suppose you want a drink?'

'I'll not refuse one,' Alvarez replied.

'And never will, until you're dead. And then, like as not, you'll sit up and open your mouth. You'd best come in.'

Alvarez entered the kitchen. It was the largest room in the house, pebble-floored, and had a vast, cowled fireplace on either side of which were bench seats. The gas cooker was a candidate for a museum, the sink had been carved out of rock, the shelves were made from sandstone; several strings of small sobrasadas hung from the ceiling. A chicken wandered in through the open doorway, then departed in a squawking hurry as it just managed to escape a boot.

Marta was preparing vegetables for the next day's market in Playa Neuva, trimming off excess stalks and leaves. She acknowledged Alvarez with a brief, toothless smile, continued working. He sat at the wooden table, its surface rippled from years of being scrubbed down. Calvo served a smoky, earthy, home-made red wine and they spoke about the crops, the drought, the stupidity of the provincial government and the incompetence of the national one.

Alvarez watched his glass tumbler as it was refilled. 'There's something you can tell me.'

'There ain't much I can't.' Calvo refilled his own glass, put down the earthenware jug on the table, turned and said to Marta: 'Some more olives.'

She slipped a rubber band over the very large lettuce in her hand, dropped the lettuce into a cane basket lined with sacking, stood slowly because her back was paining her more than usual. She crossed to one of the lower shelves beyond the sink and lifted down a jar of olives.

'D'you remember Wednesday night?' Alvarez asked.

'What if I do?'

'Who was here?'

'Me and her.'

'No one else?'

'D'you think we invite the bloody town council?'

163

Marta, who was ladling olives from the jar on to a dish, said: 'Carolina was here.'

'Of course she was.'

'It was her birthday.'

'He knows that, doesn't he?'

The foreigners had imported the idea of birthdays to be added to saints' days. An importation welcomed by the young who now tended to receive two sets of presents. 'Who's Carolina?' Alvarez asked.

'The granddaughter. Smart as they come!' said Calvo proudly. 'Last exams, she got sobresaliente in four subjects!'

Alvarez expressed the expected surprise at such brilliance at school. 'And she was the only other person here?'

'Elena,' said Marta, as she carried the jar back to the shelf. 'Her Guillermo didn't come until later on account of having to work. Arrived just before Carlos.'

However long the journey, eventually one arrived. 'Carlos Field was here?'

'Didn't I say it was Carolina's birthday?' Calvo was irritated by the other's apparent stupidity.

'Is he her godfather?'

'Wasn't on the island when she was born, so he couldn't be. They didn't make you detective because of your brains.'

'It was because of my looks ... Never have thought you'd have invited a foreigner along.'

'Are you saying I can't do as I like?'

'Enrique's not saying anything of the sort.' Marta sat, picked up a fresh lettuce, stripped off the outer leaves.

'Then what is he on about?'

She didn't answer her husband, but spoke to Alvarez: 'Don't you know?'

'What?'

She stared into space. 'She was here for the day. Loves the animals. To see her playing with a lamb ...'

'I told you she was missing,' Calvo said, with sudden force. 'I told you.'

'You said she was playing in the shed.'

'You old fool, I said nothing of the sort.'

She might not have heard. 'So I went and looked in the shed and she wasn't there. And I was terrified she'd got lost up amongst the rocks or fallen down in the cave when he was meant to be watching her, but wasn't.' She jerked her thumb in her husband's direction.

'It was you was meant to be looking after her!' he shouted.

'She'd gone the other way. Fell into the torrente what was running because of all the heavy rain. She'd've drowned if Carlos hadn't been walking along the road and heard her screaming. She'd not have had a birthday party, but for him.'

'It was your fault,' Calvo muttered. He lifted his glass and drained it, still frightened by the memory.

She slipped a rubber band around the lettuce in her hand.

Calvo went to refill his tumbler, found the jug was empty. 'More wine.'

She dropped the lettuce, stood slowly, crossed to the table, picked up the jug and left the kitchen.

Alvarez helped himself to an olive, bitter, peppery, and only a distant relative of the stuffed, tinned olives that shops sold. 'What time did the señor get here?'

'Señor? He's no señor, he's one of us.'

Most foreigners would have found that insulting as well as absurd. Alvarez could be certain that Field would understand it to be a tremendous compliment.

'How do I know when he arrived?' Calvo demanded.

Marta, who had heard the question when still outside the kitchen, entered and put the jug on the table. 'He was late and much of the food was gone, but I'd kept him some lechona because that's his favourite. Said he was late because he'd been thinking as it was his wife's birthday. Leastwise, it would have been.'

'What do you call late?'

She looked at her husband; he shrugged his shoulders.

165

'There was some salmon left and some of the cake what we'd had made specially.'

When the three of them had been young, Alvarez thought, a fiesta or a saint's day would at best have been marked by some sobrasada and a scrawny chicken. Tourism enriched lives as it destroyed living. 'You've no idea even roughly what the time was when he arrived?'

She moved one basket away, pulled another closer. 'Wasn't it just after Elena said she was leaving?' She used a knife to trim back the stalk of the green pepper that was beginning to be shot with red. 'Carlos turned up and Carolina said she wouldn't leave until she'd given "Uncle" some of her special cake. They didn't go for quite some time. It was after midnight when Guillermo said they had to leave, he was so tired.'

'The men are women these days,' Calvo said scornfully.

'Did Carlos leave then?' Alvarez asked.

'When there was plenty of drink left?'

'So how much longer did he stay?'

Marta thought it must have been at least an hour. And when they'd finally gone to bed, her husband had snored so loudly that she'd been unable to sleep properly . . .

'Always moaning!' Calvo said angrily. 'The only thing women know how to do.' He emptied the jug into their two glasses. 'More wine.'

Alvarez settled in the chair behind the desk and used a handkerchief to wipe the sweat from his forehead. There were times when life was trouble. Just before he'd left home, Dolores had said that she expected him to make Jaime come to his senses and not enter the Moors and Christians. He'd thought of pointing out that it was right to perpetuate a tradition which recorded a famous victory and that no one had been killed for several years and only a few usually suffered broken limbs, but had decided she might not find his words consoling. And what was inescapable fact was that by the evening Jaime would be a legless Moor. She had never understood that a man needed to get really tight every once in a while in order to release the pressures that were occasioned by living with a woman . . . The road to disaster began at other people's troubles. Jaime would have to work out his own solution and salvation.

He turned his mind to other matters. It was Saturday and work stopped at lunch time, provided no urgent matters arose before then. The simplest way of making sure none did was to find a legitimate reason, in itself of no complicated consequence, for being out of the office. The Cooper case could provide one such.

There were five suspects. Field had no motive and an unshakeable alibi. If White had a motive, it had so far proved impossible to uncover what it was, but in any case, he also had an unshakeable alibi. Serra had motive and whether or not he had an alibi for the revised time of death had yet to be ascertained, but it was virtually impossible to believe he possessed the degree of cunning needed to have forged the time of death. So Rachael, who had everything to gain from her husband's death, and Burns, who must hope he had everything to gain from her widowhood, were left as the prime suspects. Burns claimed they had an alibi; she had supported this. It had to be false . . .

Lady Janlin perplexed him. Her title suggested tiaras and banquets of peacocks; reality was sloppy clothes and the faint, lingering smell of plebeian cooking. Only her manner was sufficiently rude to be aristocratic.

'Of course I mind answering damn-fool questions.' She studied him. 'You don't look like a detective to me.'

'Perhaps I should leave and find a magnifying glass and a bloodhound?'

'A local with a sense of honest British humour! What'll you drink?'

'If I might have a coñac, with just ice?'

'Over there.' She pointed.

He walked around a ragged pile of newspapers and magazines on the floor, and a stool lying on its side, to reach a heavily stained cocktail cabinet. Inside was a jumble of bottles and glasses. 'What may I give you?'

'Brandy and ginger; and don't drown the brandy.'

He found two clean glasses amongst the dirty ones, a bottle of Soberano, and two ginger ales. 'Do you have some ice?'

'In the kitchen.'

He found his way to the kitchen, which was not in the state of disarray he had expected. He emptied several ice cubes from the refrigerator into a plastic bowl.

Back in the sitting-room, he handed her a glass. She drank eagerly, then said: 'Well, what does Señor Nosy Parker want?'

He sat on the settee. 'You are friendly with Señora Cooper, I understand?'

'Your understanding is correct,' she said mockingly.

'When did you last see her?'

'Damned if I can remember.'

'I am investigating the murder of Señor Cooper.'

'So?'

'I need to know where the señora was on Wednesday night.'

'You think she might have killed Oliver? What if she did? Justifiable homicide.'

'The law must hold otherwise.'

'I've known too many lawyers to have any respect for the law.'

'It's not always that one can afford such a luxury.'

'The world's not made for small people.' She drained her glass. 'I'll have another; and less ginger.'

He wondered, as he put his own glass down on the corner of an occasional table, whether her vocabulary included the word 'please'? He refilled her glass and handed it back. 'I have to know where the señora was.'

'Here.'

'On her own?'

'With that man she's seeing. God knows why. Slumming can be amusing, but never for very long. He may be a hunk of testosterone, but that's the limit of his attractions.'

'Neil Burns was here with the señora on Wednesday night?'

'Do I need to repeat everything I say if you're ever to understand?'

'When did they arrive?'

She shrugged her shoulders.

'You cannot give even an estimate of the time?'

'I choose to live on this island in order to forget time.'

'Was it dark?'

'God knows.'

'Then it could have been after eleven?'

'No.'

'Why not?'

'They were here when I rang my bastard husband and I had to wait until ten thirty to get hold of him because he was doing good works somewhere. When he dies, God will have to move over.'

169

'When did Señor Burns leave here?'

'When he went.'

'Could it have been before midnight?'

'When there's free booze around, his bum goes numb.'

'I'm not certain I understand what that means.'

'Then it's a pity you never learned English.'

'Or that you learned Spanish.'

She laughed. 'I'm beginning to like you! Not at all the plump little erk you look.'

He was sorry that Spanish manners precluded him from pointing out that when it came to size, she had the advantage in many areas. 'Roughly, when did Señor Burns leave here?'

'One o'clock; two o'clock; three o'clock, knock.'

'Not before midnight?'

'That's sharp; that's right!'

He hesitated. She was amused by him and therefore was regarding him good-naturedly. But if he annoyed her, she would almost certainly become pure bitch. Yet if he didn't challenge her, he would never be certain. He took a deep breath. 'Lady Janlin, that cannot be correct. I know that Señor Burns was not in this house all the time between ten thirty and midnight.'

Her manner did not sharpen; if anything, she became even more offhand. 'Really?' she drawled.

He bluffed with all the conviction he could command. 'I have spoken to a witness who saw him in his car after eleven and before midnight.'

'My good man, that's quite impossible. Suggest your witness adds more water next time.'

'Do you understand that in this country it is a serious crime deliberately to mislead a police officer?'

'You're beginning to remind me of my pompous husband and that's bad for my digestion.'

He stood. 'I offer you one more chance to tell the truth.'

'He'd never offer anybody anything, so the similarity is not all that close.' She drained her glass and held it out.

'You know the definition of a gentleman? He pours a lady a drink even when he's not trying to seduce her.'

He tried to work out whether it would be safer to refill her glass or flee.

CHAPTER 23

The fiesta of Llueso was spaced over several days; on the Saturday night, there was dancing in the old square to a live band whose music was amplified until only those who lived on the outskirts of the village had any hope of sleeping during the night unless the members of the band became totally inebriated.

The mobile churro stall was doing almost as much trade as the cafés which surrounded the square and it was five minutes before Alvarez was able to buy a small bag of the crisp, deep-fried, ribbed lengths of pastry-like sweet. He eased his way through the milling crowds until he found a space, began to eat. Taste, smell, and music, resurrected the past in a flash of time. He knew a pain that had never vanished, only dulled. The last time he had escorted Juana-María to a fiesta. There had been few tourists then and money had been so tight that the band had consisted of three villagers who only occasionally had managed to play together and in tune; mothers had watched their daughters with eagle eyes; the churro stall had been small and mobile only to the extent that two men could push it; Juana-María and he had bought a bag of churros and she had said that if there were an odd number of pieces in it, she would know that he truly loved her, but if there were an even number . . . When he'd wanted to eat quickly, she had held the bag tightly shut, laughing with the abandon that came from pure happiness and causing her mother to chide her for brazenness . . . A little while later, she had died, pinned against a wall by a car driven by a drunken Frenchman . . .

Someone spoke to him, but his thoughts were too far

172

away and the noise too great for him either to recognize the voice or understand the words. He turned and to his surprise found himself facing Rachael.

'I saw you . . .' she began, but the band scaled fresh heights. She shrugged her shoulders, mouthed words as she pointed to the road past the Club Llueso. She set off and he followed her. Halfway down the road, the buildings masked the noise sufficiently for normal speech to be audible. She came to a stop. 'I saw you only at the very last moment.'

He replied, with conventional triteness: 'It's very crowded because a lot of tourists come here for the fiesta.'

'Frankly, you obviously hadn't seen me so I was about to rush off, reckoning it was a meeting neither of us would welcome. But then I thought . . .'

'You thought what, señora?'

'Rachael! I thought that perhaps the best thing to do was to face you here and now and have it out.'

'I don't understand.'

'Muriel rang me and said you'd virtually been accusing Neil . . .'

'Señora, this . . .'

'Rachael, goddamnit!'

'This is hardly the time or place to discuss such a matter.'

'I don't give a shit! I must make you understand that neither Neil nor I had anything to do with Oliver's death.'

'Come to my office on Monday.'

'Come home now and listen. You owe me that for being so horribly suspicious. Please, you've got to.'

The telephone call from Lady Janlin had panicked her, he thought. Panicky tongues could be provoked into speaking freely. But by Monday she would have calmed down and worked out how to meet the fresh challenge.

She settled on the settee. With her legs tucked under herself, her dress riding some way up her thighs, and her hair slightly dishevelled, she looked vulnerable, younger, and very desirable.

She drank quickly. She said in a low voice: 'I've been lying to you.' She looked up and directly at him. 'About Neil and me. But you'd guessed the truth. When you found me in his flat, I could see in your face that you didn't believe what we told you.'

'You're admitting that your affair with him did not come to an end a long time ago?'

'Yes.' She studied him as if seeking to discover something. 'You know, don't you, that sometimes between two people there's an electrical current that blasts them into another world and they forget all loyalties, duties, and self-respect?'

He did not answer.

'Come on, admit you're not the stolid, unemotional man you try to make out.'

'When did Señor Cooper discover you were having an affair?'

'Since it would never have occurred to him that I'd ever be more than distantly polite to someone in Neil's lowly position, and I made certain I was the soul of discretion, he remained in complete and happy ignorance of the fact.'

'You are still lying.'

'I swear I'm not.'

'He learned the truth and threatened to divorce you. Since he was living on this island and all his money was offshore from England, there was no way you could get any court to force him to pay you maintenance. And you knew that since you'd made him a laughing stock by cuckolding him, he'd never willingly give you so much as a peseta.'

'What are you implying now?'

'That you had the strongest possible motive for his murder.'

'He didn't know!' she shouted. 'You think I'd murder him for his money? Oh, God, how can you be so cruel? Why are you horribly twisting everything I say? Why won't you . . . ?'

The cordless phone on the table by her side rang, bringing an abrupt end to her words. She stared at it, but made no effort to pick it up. Her expression slowly calmed.

Alvarez silently cursed the caller. Fear had undermined her self-control, as he had intended; but this interruption had given her the time to realize that at all costs she must regain it. The ringing ceased. He said: 'Where were you at eleven o'clock Wednesday evening?'

'Muriel's told you I was with her.'

'She also said Señor Burns was in her house until the early hours of Thursday morning. I know that he was not.'

'You know nothing!' She drained her glass. 'I asked you here to show you why you had to stop suspecting Neil and me. But all you –'

The phone interrupted her again. This time, she picked it up. 'Yes, Charles? . . . I couldn't get to it in time . . . There's no need to apologize . . . That is an idea. It would certainly help me to sort out that side of things . . . The Poperens? Of course you can have them. You know I've never liked them and, after all, you did paint them . . . At around eleven, then. Good night.' She replaced the phone on the table, stood. 'It's time for a refill.'

He handed her his glass. As she walked over to the cocktail cabinet, she said: 'Understand this. I'm no starry-eyed romantic. Even when the electricity flashed, I recognized that what started so suddenly would end equally suddenly.' She turned, walked towards him, a glass in each hand. 'So there was never the slightest possibility of a long-term relationship and without that, Neil would never risk his neck by murdering Oliver.'

She came to a stop immediately in front of him.

'Money usually outlives romance.'

'Neil doesn't have the prescience to understand that. He is an uncomplicated character and for him there's only the present.'

'Unlike you?'

'I'm far more complex. Which means that if I had plotted and planned, I'd also have considered every possibility there was for failure and that would have made me far too scared actually to put any of the plots and plans into execution.' She handed him his glass, leaning forward far more than was necessary.

Her dress had a deep décolletage and inevitably his attention was drawn. She was not wearing a brassiere and the upper curves of her shapely breasts were visible. He hastily jerked his gaze away before she caught him peeping. Yet as she straightened up, her quiet smile said that his subterfuge had been a complete waste of time and effort because with infallible female instinct she had divined where his gaze had been focused a moment before; her smile also said – to his surprised excitement – that she was neither annoyed nor contemptuous.

She returned to the settee; as she settled, her skirt rode higher up her thighs than before and again she made no attempt to tug it down. 'Do you understand now that we couldn't have had anything to do with Oliver's death?' When he did not answer, she said: 'Christ! Have I got to bare every last inch of my soul to convince you?'

He waited.

She plucked at the hem of her dress. 'Promise you won't become all holier-than-thou if I admit something?'

'I try never to do that.'

'On the Wednesday, all Neil and I did together was have a meal and then go straight to Muriel's – I told him before we drove to the restaurant that it was all finished between us. So he knew there wasn't any future and couldn't have any reason to kill Oliver.'

'Why did you tell him your relationship was finished?'

'In one respect, I'm the same as Neil.'

'Is that an answer?'

'Dammit, you're making me dot the i's and cross the t's because you're enjoying making me squirm.'

'That's ridiculous.'

'Then if you're not being deliberately slow, you aren't very good at judging people. I . . . I've always needed excitement to make life worth living. And the most exciting

176

thing of all is to meet someone new and face the questions: will he, and if he does, will I?'

She was staring straight at him, her eyes wide, her lips slightly parted, the tip of her tongue just visible, her body tensed. He would have had to be a dolt not to have understood. She had set out to convince him of her and Burns's innocence by an apparent show of total innocence. Failing, she had judged her position to be serious. She saw one way of escape. He had been unable to hide his lascivious interest in her. Then let him believe her, or at the very least accept that she had been the unwilling and unwitting partner, and she would offer affirmative answers to the questions he had just posed.

He longed to say he now believed her. His mind even provided Jesuitical justification for doing so. By seducing him in order to make him forget his duty towards the law he was supposed to serve, she would be proving herself to be corrupt; then it would not be unfair if his agreement, knowing he would not subsequently allow himself to be diverted from doing his job, were equally corrupt. Yet to accept such reasoning would be to betray himself, and the most precious thing a man possessed was his self-respect.

He finished his drink, said goodbye, and left.

CHAPTER 24

Monday was a ghastly day; midday Saturday was a long, long way away.

Alvarez stared at the pile of papers, memoranda and unopened letters on his desk and gloomily decided that he must sort out everything, even taking action over those that were very important.

A cabo opened the door and looked into the room. 'So you've finally decided to turn up! Better late than never, as the puta said when Lent came to an end.'

'I've already put in a couple of hours' work.'

'Cows might growl. This came in for you during the night.' He entered the room to place a fax on the desk. 'Don't work yourself to death or you'll live to regret it,' he said cheerfully, before leaving.

Youth was a time of irrational optimism. Alvarez decided to go to the Club Llueso for a second breakfast in the hopes that a quick coñac would cheer him up; then, ever the man who observed duty, he read the fax.

America reported that Ernest White had been born in Philadelphia to Italian parents. He had had youthful convictions for gang-related offences; in adult life he had matriculated to major crime, but had been convicted only once and imprisoned for five years. Presently believed to be an enforcer for the Ruggiero crime syndicate. The authorities would be grateful for any information concerning his present activities.

Alvarez put the fax down, left the office. The old square was thronged with people, mostly foreigners with nothing to do but eat and drink, and he had to weave his way between them so that by the time he reached the Club

Llueso he was sweating freely. The barman said that he looked like a man about to have a fatal heart attack.

He sat at a table by the window and drank some of the coffee, then topped up the cup with brandy. He lit a cigarette. Since White could not be the murderer, the reason for his having visited Cooper became immaterial. Nevertheless, America had asked for information and a drive over to Cala Xima was far preferable to sitting at a desk, sorting through papers . . .

The brunette, dressed in the briefest of bikinis, stared up at Alvarez with open resentment.

'Back home,' White said, snapping the words short, 'I'd have a mouthpiece suing you for harassment.'

'Then I must count myself fortunate that this is Spain.'

'What the goddamn hell is it this time?'

'I have received information from America.'

White's expression became blank.

'Perhaps we could go inside and discuss it?'

White turned to his companion. 'I've got to talk to this guy.'

'But why . . . ?' she began.

'Grab another bottle and charge it to my room.'

She looked round for the nearest waiter.

The two men, Alvarez in the rear, went round the pool and through into the cool lounge; this time, unoccupied until their arrival.

'Well?' demanded White.

'America says you have a record.'

'So?'

'And that you are an enforcer for a crime syndicate.'

'Moonbeams.'

'So I've been asking myself, what were you persuading Señor Cooper to do, or not to do?'

A waiter started towards the table, turned aside when waved away.

'You can't finger me,' said White. 'I was here, in this hotel, when he was wasted.'

179

'Perhaps you could not have been directly involved in his death, but I think you arranged it. And as proof of that is the fact that you made certain you had an alibi both for the apparent time of death and the actual time.'

'I'm guilty because I've an alibi? Even a dick back home would find that dumb.'

'So unless you tell me what happened, and why, I shall have to arrest you as a material witness who refuses to cooperate.'

'I'll have the sharpest mouthpiece in the land shouting . . .'

'He can shout as loudly as he likes, señor, but it will be to no effect. A material witness is obliged to reveal any evidence of which he has knowledge – not even American citizenship allows exemption . . . Since I can prove through eyewitness evidence that you were keeping observation on Ca'n Oliver through binoculars and this, prima facie, suggests a nefarious intention, it has to be reasonable to assume you know something of considerable consequence to the investigation. It is, then, up to you to rebut such assumption, perhaps by showing that the reason for your surveillance and your visit to the señor had neither direct nor indirect connection with the señor's death. However, if you continue to refuse to cooperate, it will be my duty to arrest you so that you may be questioned further. It could then take you a very long time to gain your freedom – assuming you will be entitled to do so. It has been said that only the dead move as slowly as the Spanish legal system.'

White's expression was no longer blank, but ugly.

'Let me ask you once more so that you have the chance to avoid much unpleasantness: Why did you keep watch on Ca'n Oliver? Why did you visit Señor Cooper, whom you had never met before?'

There was a long silence. Finally, White said: 'He owed money.'

'To whom?'

'Someone.'

'How much?'

'One million, three hundred and fifty grand.'

'In what currency?'

'Dollars.' He spoke as if no other currency were possible.

'Why did he owe this money?'

'He sold a couple of paintings which later turned out to be fakes.'

'So the buyer wanted his money back?'

'Wouldn't you?'

'Why did he not go through the usual legal channels?'

White did not answer.

'The paintings were bought with black money so that it was impossible to sue in open court?'

'Work it out for yourself.'

'You told him to pay up or suffer the consequences?'

'I advised him.'

'Presumably, he saw that as good advice, but difficult to act on?'

White said harshly: 'It was in the interests of the person I represent for Cooper to go on living.'

'Yes, I realize that,' Alvarez replied slowly. He also realized several other things.

He drove slowly, his thoughts more on the case than the road.

For many years, members of organized crime syndicates had laundered their black money by investing in legitimate enterprises; recently, they had turned to art as an investment. Ironically, this had bred the mirror image of prideful boasting to be found amongst most legitimate collectors which had led to their pursuing ever more avidly the better paintings.

Cooper had been commissioned to find and buy some valuable paintings. The art world was an enclosed one in which gossip charged fact and fact, gossip. He had learned enough to judge, and perhaps instinct had partially told him, that the unnamed purchaser was a wealthy American criminal. Such a purchaser was a sucker waiting to be taken. Regarding any purchase as an investment rather than a work of genius so that instinctive taste would never cause him to doubt, he dare not reveal his ownership of the painting except to close friends, far less to put it on the market for many years, so that the chances of its being identified as a fake during such time as this would be dangerous to the seller were almost nil.

Cooper had known Field, a brilliant restorer and copyist for many years. Field was in money troubles because of his wife's long illness and so was likely to be open to making by unorthodox means the money he so desperately needed. Cooper had bought two genuine Poperens. Field had copied these, Cooper had sold the fakes and what they had fetched, together with the sale of the gallery, had made him a rich man. He had kept the genuine Poperens because a) it would be an act of total folly to put them on the market, b) he possessed a very strong sense of proprietary interest in the works because it was he who had done so much to establish the artist's greatly enhanced standing and c) they provided the secret, perverted pleasure which came from enjoying something denied to others.

The world was such a small place that if the paintings were hung in his own house – which they had to be for safety's sake and his pleasure – the odds were that someone who visited the house would identify them as those supposedly sold in America. So he'd hidden them in the safest possible way – in full view, labelled copies. (Remember the sexually active figures in the corners. When he had remarked on their brilliant execution, Field had bitterly said that his copies were only a shadow of the originals; Field had known that the praise was for work which possessed that extra quality which only genius could provide and which his must always lack.)

When White had turned up, Cooper's smooth, luxurious world had suddenly been shattered, as he was faced with either handing over one million three hundred and fifty thousand dollars or suffering physical brutality, perhaps death. He had chosen to mix with a set where wealth was

God and therefore if reduced to what, by their lights, would be poverty, he must become an object of scorn; even the threat of physical violence turned his bowels to water. A clever man, if pompously self-satisfied, panic had helped him to work out a way of escape. Short-term, he would set a scene of suicide which appeared to have been sufficiently mishandled to suggest murder – then people (and White in particular) would be far less likely to believe he was not really dead. Long-term, he'd leave the island and settle somewhere fresh, making certain he could not be traced. But whilst it was safe to leave the house to be sold at a later date, whereupon the money and Rachael could catch up with him, all the time the two Poperens were not in his physical possession, they – and his innocence – must be at risk, or so his panicky mind had assured him; the possibility of someone else's acquiring them and discovering his fraud was one he could not contemplate. So when he had deemed it safe to do so, he had returned at night to Ca'n Oliver, expecting Rachael to be there so that he could explain everything, tell her what to do, and get her to help him load the paintings into the van he'd hired. What he had not foreseen was that ironically she would not be at home because his faked death had given her the green light to pursue her affair. Finding the house empty, he'd turned for help to the one man he believed would give it without the possibility of any risk to himself.

Field had never been a serious suspect. First, because it had always seemed that he lacked any motive for the murder. How could he gain from killing the only man who was prepared to help him attain his burning ambition? But the truth was that he'd known the two Poperens were genuine and worth a fortune and that Rachael (whose values were always financial) disliked them because she believed them to be worthless. (Cooper would never have told her the truth when this was not necessary, since to do so would have been to identify himself as a crook; a man of his character always needed to believe that in the eyes of others he was cause for envy, not contempt.) So

Field had known that if Cooper died, a fortune would become his merely by persuading Rachael to give him the two 'copies'. Secondly, he had made certain he had had no alibi for the time of death as set by the broken watch. The psychology of that move had been spot on. When the revised time of death had been set, it had seemed he had to be innocent. But just in case, and to sew everything up, he'd provided himself with an unshakeable alibi for the actual time of death.

The Mallorquin character had been summed up as quiet hostility towards all without, total loyalty to all within. When Field had saved Carolina from possible death by drowning, he had become a member of the Calvo family. So when he'd asked them for an alibi, they had not hesitated to give this. Challenge them, call them liars, plead with them to tell the truth in the name of justice, threaten them with the law's penalties for false testimony, and they would stare vacantly into space. They would forever observe the one truth – no sacrifice was too great for one's family. It was this that had enabled the islanders to survive centuries of invasion, persecution, and poverty. It made Alvarez proud to recognize the limitless boundaries of their loyalty to their own. It made him swear because it was going to be very, very difficult to uncover the outside evidence that would prove Field to be the murderer.

CHAPTER 25

'You're serious when you accuse me of murdering Oliver?'
Field sounded more surprised than anything.

'I am,' Alvarez replied. 'You knew the two paintings
were genuine, not fakes.'

'That is possibly true.'

'And that they are worth over a million dollars.'

'Probably well over, by now. Oliver was convinced that
Poperen's works will continue to rise steadily in value.'

'They represent a lot of money.'

'In my financial dictionary, a fortune.'

'Which you decided you could steal without any risk to
yourself because only you and Señor Cooper knew that
the paintings on the wall were genuine. Since Señora
Cooper had no idea of their true worth, believing them to
be copies painted by you, and did not even like them, once
Señor Cooper was dead she would be happy to give them
to you to get them out of the way.'

'An ingenious theory. But aren't you overlooking something? At the time of Oliver's death, I was at Carolina's
party.'

'If you ask the Calvo family to lie for you, they will lie.
They are lying when they say you were in their house
throughout the time.'

'Can you prove that?'

'The surrounding circumstances will make it clear that
the court is entitled to draw the inference that the Calvos
are committing perjury because they feel under the obliga-
tion to do so.'

'What surrounding circumstances?'

'The fact that on Señor Cooper's death the only person

who knew the worth of the two paintings was you; that instead of telling Señora Cooper the truth about them, you have persuaded her to give them to you in the belief that they are worthless.'

'You would hold, then, that it is motive which forges the proof against me?'

'Motive usually does.'

'Then suppose I tell you that I have offered, as a gift, one painting to the Prado and the other to the National Gallery, neither of which possesses a Poperen?'

Alvarez did not try to hide his surprise and consternation.

'Perhaps you don't believe me? Then ask the directors to confirm the offer ... I'm sure you'll be the first to appreciate that if I had no intention of gaining from my unique knowledge concerning the paintings, my motive for murdering Oliver cannot be financial. So why should I have killed him when I owed him so much and I had reason to hope I would soon owe him more? And one final point. I didn't tell Rachael the truth about the paintings because I did know she'd been having an affair. In the circumstances, I was damned if I was going to see her enjoying a further fortune from his estate.'

Alvarez slowly accepted the logic. With no motive for the murder, Field could not be the murderer.

'Now, just to show you that I've no hard feelings over being falsely accused, let me offer you a drink – coñac and ice, as last time?'

Alvarez entered the dining-room, sat. He stared at the almost-empty bottle of brandy on the table. 'Have you got the other?'

Jaime reached under the table and brought up a second bottle, half full. Alvarez poured himself a drink.

'Pass the bottle back,' Jaime said urgently.

'She's still on the warpath?'

'Worse than ever. And I don't care what she says, it wasn't my fault.'

'What wasn't?'

'That I tripped over something and fell against that print she bought at the fair last year and made such a fuss about. If it had been a decent frame, it wouldn't have bust when it fell on to the floor. She's shouting that I've got to get it reframed. I tell you one thing, if I decide to do that, I'll let Eduardo know exactly what I think of his work. He bloody well ought to make the frames solid enough to stand falling on the floor without busting. I said to her, I can knock the slivers of wood back into place with some tacks, but she wouldn't listen. Never does . . .'

Slivers of wood. A sliver of wood in the dead man's wounds. Someone whom Alvarez was certain was the murderer, yet whose character seemed to deny the possibility; who was a brilliant copyist, but who yearned to be a true artist. A man who had been assured by Cooper that he could and would become a true artist, even though his work seemed to have little merit; a man who had trusted Cooper. A stout frame, a torn canvas . . .

Alvarez accepted that almost certainly he would never be able to prove the truth. But he was now reasonably certain that he knew what that was. After Cooper had faked his suicide/murder, he had holed up in one of the small 'assignation' hotels or hostels where a ten-thousand-peseta note produced total amnesia amongst the staff. Then, as soon as he'd believed it safe to do so, he'd hired a small van and booked passage on the morning ferry, gambling on what he believed to be a certainty – he'd never doubted his own cleverness – that the police would be on the lookout for his murderer, not him. He had returned to Ca'n Oliver that Wednesday night to retrieve the two Poperens and brief Rachael. Which was when his plans had started to go wrong. She had not been there. Panicking, he'd telephoned Field for help. As soon as he'd understood the position, Field had responded to what most concerned him at this point – what was to happen re his paintings; Cooper would, wouldn't he, continue whenever possible to do everything in his power to promote them?

Cooper, terrified that all the time he was in the house he was at risk – probably crediting White with near-supernatural powers and therefore likely to turn up at any moment – had cut short Field's queries and pleas by brutally telling him the truth. His work wasn't good enough even to adorn the lid of a biscuit tin . . .

Hell hath no fury like an artist scorned. Yet Field had not just been scorned, he had seen himself betrayed and his ambition strangled – an ambition that was entwined with memories of, and homage to, his beloved wife. In his agonized fury, probably so great that he had not fully realized what he was doing, he'd stormed through to the bedroom in which the painting he'd given Cooper had been banished, wrenched it off the wall, returned and smashed it repeatedly down on Cooper's head.

He had regained a measure of self-control. Faced with the fact that he had killed and, if nothing were done to conceal this, he must be convicted of murder, he had set out to false-fake the time of death in such a way as eventually to establish his innocence after initially pointing to his guilt, confident that there was every chance that sooner or later Gore's evidence – he'd been at the house when the phone call had been made – would prove that Cooper had been alive at eleven. He had taken his shattered painting with him, driven off in the hired vehicle in which Cooper had arrived; he had abandoned it, knowing that this was a sufficiently common occurrence amongst the more inebriated foreigners that it would arouse no special comment. Once home, he'd burned the shattered frame, which had left the sliver of varnished wood in the dead man's head, but not the canvas, because even if it had been torn and therefore bore witness to the savage assault, he could not consign his own work to the flames. (Fresh paint had replaced the bloodstains.) Later, he had offered the two Poperens to the museums, partially because by doing so he could, despite failure, find artistic success of a kind – his name as donor would be remembered . . .

Alvarez's thoughts were interrupted.

'Have you gone into a trance?' Jaime demanded.

Alvarez drained his glass. 'I was thinking.'

'What about?'

He refilled his glass after Jaime had passed him the bottle. 'The murder.'

'The woman in the swimming pool? Not seen her in the nude, have you?'

'I could have done.'

'You're a bloody liar!'

He dropped ice cubes into his glass. 'On Saturday night, she asked me back to her place. She offered it on a plate.'

Jaime leaned forward. 'So what was it like?'

'I was so certain she was mixed up in the murder, I reckoned that on ethical grounds I had to refuse. But you know what? It's turned out that she didn't have anything to do with that so I could have gone right ahead. Ironic, isn't it?'

Jaime described the incident in different terms.